Music Master

by

Barbara Jean Miller

Music Master

Cover Art by *Jennifer Greeff*

The Wild Rose Press, Inc.
PO Box 708
Adams Basin, NY 14410-0708
Visit us at www.thewildrosepress.com

Publishing History
First Edition, 2023
Trade Paperback ISBN 978-1-5092-5237-4
Digital ISBN 978-1-5092-5238-1

Published in the United States of America

"Be serious, Leighton. You are wounded," she said, grasping him by the cravat and scrutinizing his face. Something happened then. Some unspoken word passed between them and she hesitated as she saw him raise himself enough to kiss her. Not only that, he drew her to his chest as she got lost in her single-minded desire to be close to him. She felt open, in accord with him, as though all the constraint of their many separations had been banished. Moreover, she felt an intense longing for him. Had the effort of keeping away from him created this flood tide of passion? His kiss was hungry and demanding, and she wanted to taste him in return. When she finally drew back, she stared at him in amazement.

"What just happened?" she asked, her lips throbbing and a deep ache of longing growing inside her chest.

"This is what I have been trying to tell you since I met you today." Leighton shook his head and grinned at her. "I love you."

"But Leighton." She pulled back and tried to escape his arms. "You do not fall in love in an instant," she scoffed.

"But I have always loved you. You said it yourself—we are not children anymore. We are perfect together."

"Perfect? We won't be allowed." Maddie struggled in his arms, feeling like a rabbit in a snare, then stilled. It *would* be perfect. As she gazed at Leighton, he raised his head and kissed her again, his lips warm and tender. With her eyes closed like this and his arms around her, she could imagine, for once, being his wife, being with him always.

Praise for Barbara Jean Miller

"*MUSIC MASTER* by Barbara Miller is historical storytelling at its best. Maddie and Leighton are compelling characters that readers will greatly enjoy. The plot is fast-paced and engaging and full of surprises. *MUSIC MASTER* is a story that reminded me of why I love reading. I highly recommend it."

~*Two Lips Reviews*

~*~

"*MUSIC MASTER* is a well-crafted story with very engaging characters. The added backdrop of the Napoleonic Wars helps bring this story to life, adding depth to the characters and color to the story.... Readers will quickly find themselves rooting for this couple to succeed and for the author to write a sequel."

~*Coffee Time Romance Reviews*

Dedication

For my hero and husband Don.
Without him there would be no books.

Chapter One

England, Summer 1814

Leighton scanned the new green of the hayfield from the back of his cantering horse. Jasper pricked his ears forward at sight of the hedge where they used to jump when hunting foxes or hares with the squire's son. But that was years ago, before the war in the Peninsula, before the death of Leighton's father, and before these arguments with his mother sent him riding away in frustration. Home from London only a few hours and already they had quarreled.

"What do you think, Jasper? Can you still do it?" He nudged the horse toward the hedge and Jasper turned eagerly. "All right. Hup!"

The hunter almost leaped from under him in its joyful spring. They covered the distance to the hedgerow in great ground-eating strides, Jasper's shoes biting into the springy turf and throwing up clods of grass. Leighton felt the horse's muscles bunch between his thighs, got the soaring elation of flying, and heard the swish of greenery under Jasper's belly. Then he glimpsed a flash of gray that should not have been behind the hedgerow. Jasper saw it too and stopped short on landing, sending his rider somersaulting over his head to land with a breathless thud onto the grassy lane. Leighton found himself staring up into the startled green eyes of Maddie Westlake in her gray cloak.

"Leighton, are you hurt?" She dropped her basket and pushed the hood back from her brown ringlets to grab for Jasper's bridle. "Let go of the reins!" she commanded Leighton.

Leighton gasped for air as he ascertained she was unharmed, then saw Jasper's feet dancing nervously near his head. He uncurled his fingers, rolled out of the way, and scrambled to his feet. "Maddie, I am so sorry! I nearly landed on top of you."

"It is my fault. I surprised him by being too near the hedge." Maddie stroked Jasper's muzzle. When the horse bowed its head, she scratched its ears. Leighton watched the animal rest its forehead against her breast as though it had missed her as much as he had.

Maddie looked up at him and smiled. "We are lucky he has better sense than both of us."

"Better eyes, at any rate." Leighton stood gingerly and dusted himself off, noting that he would have a bruised shoulder for his carelessness but nothing more serious. Then he stooped to examine Jasper's legs.

"You had better walk him," Maddie advised. "If he stove a knee, it is better to find out before riding him again."

"You are a sensible girl," Leighton said, beginning to lead the horse and looking behind to observe the animal's gait and make sure he was not lame.

"It doesn't take much sense to care for a horse."

She picked up her large basket and began walking beside him, her worn shoes peeking from beneath the dusty edge of her work skirt. Obviously none of the money he had sent her to take care of his older tenants had been squandered on herself. That would change now that he was able to marry her.

Maddie had the most delicate feet, and she was a head shorter than he, but one word from Maddie was like a command. He always did what she said because she was so sensible.

"Most women would have fallen over in a dead faint or gone into hysterics at almost being run down. Whereas you—"

"Expect it from you?" she supplied in her low matter-of-fact voice, the corners of her generous mouth turning up in the hint of a smile.

He studied her lips almost the color of strawberries and remembered tasting those lips the last summer things had been normal, six years ago. "I forgot how sharp your tongue can be. I have been missing this, I think. Let me carry that basket home for you." He reached for it and touched her hand on the handle. He had the distinct feeling that she would not have surrendered her burden except to avoid contact with him. She was the same Maddie, yet he felt distanced from her and he didn't know why.

"Are you back for good then?" she asked, staring at the ground and clasping her hands together as they walked on.

"From London? Yes, now that Napoleon has been shipped off to Elba, they do not need me at the Foreign Office. There is the estate to look after." He swung the basket and wondered at its weight.

"I never understood what you did there," she said, stooping to pick a daisy from the middle of the lane.

He watched her twirl it between her fingers. It was early summer, he had just gotten home from London, it was now safe to declare himself, but he did not know how to begin. "I did not understand it all myself." A lie was not a good beginning, but secrecy gets to be such a habit that the truth is the last thing you think to tell someone, even someone you love.

"So you wrote dispatches?"

"No, not from London. All that happens at the front. I just…clerked."

"It must have been important, to keep you away three parts of the year."

"In war everything is important."

"Not just in war." She looked away toward the churchyard and the vicarage.

"I know. Do you think I do not realize how hard it has been for you? Doing the visits and keeping faith with the old people, when it is my mother who should be taking care of them."

"Sometimes your sister comes with me in her gig. Amy feels the same as you, but she has children."

"With her children to care for, the burden of looking after the old cottagers has fallen on you."

"It is no burden, and that was not what I meant by everything. You could have broken your neck just a few moments ago. It doesn't even concern you." Maddie's eyes glistened with belated tears. That was Maddie, always as cool as ice during an emergency but feeling it to the extreme later.

Leighton watched a flush of embarrassment kiss her cheek and wished he had a free hand to brush her concern away. "I was more worried about you."

"Why? Do you feel responsible for me because you grant my father his living?" she asked.

"What? No. There has always been a Westlake in the vicarage at Longbridge. I was concerned because I care about you. I have since we were children."

"We are past childish cares, all grown up now. No more picking flowers." She tossed the bloom away. "Or riding our ponies to the village. No more stealing strawberries from the garden. We are adults now and must not look back."

"Why not? My best memories are of you," Leighton said, thinking of strawberry juice on those ripe lips, remembering bringing Maddie the best berries because she liked them so much. "Everything that was good happened in the past."

This brought a frown to her countenance, and on Maddie it looked tragic. She turned her face away.

Now Leighton regretted making her sad. "When I saw you at church last Christmas I got the feeling you are not happy."

"Happy?" she asked, directing a confused look at him. "I've never thought about it."

She said it rapidly, in that way she had when trying to hide something. She increased the pace of her walk, but he had no trouble keeping up with her small strides.

"You have a right to happiness—more right than many I know. You should not be working so hard, carrying heavy things," he complained, then hefted the large market basket. "What is in here, anyway? It weighs a ton."

"A dead cat," Maddie said briefly.

"A what?" Leighton dropped the burden and stared at the old rag covering it as though he didn't believe her. Jasper almost walked into him.

"Old Mrs. Horwith's dead cat. She is too old to bury him and could not bear to do it even if she were able. Since I will pass the cemetery on the way home, I promised to get a shovel from the caretaker's tool shed and inter the beast."

Leighton stared at her. "That seems above and beyond the call of even a dutiful vicar's daughter."

"Someone has to. Well, are you bringing it?"

Leighton shrugged and picked up the loathsome burden. "Your average dewy-eyed miss would have a cabbage and a bunch of carrots in her basket, but you are sure to have something like a dead cat."

Maddie opened her mouth as if to argue with him but said only, "I am not dewy-eyed."

"But Maddie, you are a beautiful woman, whether you are aware of it or not."

She shot him an accusing look, almost a scowl, then shook her head as though trying to school her expression into a more polite frame. She succeeded only in freeing some stray tendrils of hair from the ribbon at the back of her head. Leighton watched in fascination as they curled against her cheek.

"I hear your sister Susan is to go to London to make her debut," she said as though trying to change the subject.

"Mother wanted it this year, but with the war, things were too uncertain. I preferred to delay Susan's come out. Would you like to go to London? You have never been there." He was thinking that with Maddie as his wife, next season would be enjoyable. To get from here to there he had to propose to her, but it was damned difficult to woo a woman when you were carrying a dead cat.

"What would be the point—I mean, I cannot. I have to take care of the vicarage and the church. Also the cemetery."

"But that is not your responsibility, surely." Leighton looked out over the huddled rows of stones, some so old the carving had been completely worn away by rain.

"Old Masham scythes it, but he doesn't trim around the stones."

They came to the small shed at the edge of the cemetery and Maddie unlocked it, handing a pick and shovel out to Leighton. He dropped Jasper's reins over the cast-iron fence and took the tools from her.

"Your sisters are both married now," Leighton said.

"Yes, I'm all alone with Papa."

"I still say you could use a holiday. If London does not appeal to you, there is Brighton, or—"

"Leighton, are you mad? There is too much to do. Besides, what purpose would it serve?"

"You are not making this easy. What I am trying to ask you—"

"Leighton, please let us bury the cat. Then you can ask me anything you like."

He could see the advantage of disposing of the corpse first. "Is this that huge old tabby that used to hiss at us and strike at our legs from under the table?"

"The very one. He must be nearly as old as I am. Do cats live to be twenty?"

"Not normally. Allow me the pleasure of digging the hole for you. I can't count the number of times he's laid my hand open."

She looked him up and down. "You'll get your boots all muddy."

"I do not mind a bit of mud," he said and slid through a broken part of the fence, then prepared to excavate a grave at the edge of the pauper's section.

"Not in consecrated ground, you idiot. Dig out here in the woods a bit." Maddie took a few steps to a small clearing and scraped away the leaves with one dainty foot, commanding Leighton to dig.

He loved the endearing way she called him an idiot. Surely they were fated to be together. "I suppose you are right. I do not think this cat was a Christian." Leighton set the basket down, took off his hat and coat, and hung them on a limb before he began loosening the earth with the pick.

Maddie stared out over her domain. Leighton thought it terrible that such a young, vital creature was so tied to the dead. He would change that.

"My mother's stone is over there," she whispered, staring in the direction of the cemetery.

"Yes, carried off by a fever almost overnight." Leighton paused in his task. "Then to hear that my father was lost at sea… I wonder why he took a notion to go visit his brother in America? He never knew she died."

"I never knew you had an uncle."

"Neither did I. The letter he left explained that William was a natural son of my grandfather." Leighton cast the pick aside and began to scoop out the loose earth with the spade, enjoying the satisfying scrape of metal against earth and rock. The dirt smelled wonderfully alive and fecund, as though it was eager to grow something. Ironic that they would be giving it something dead. But irony was part of the cycle too.

"You were at university," Maddie said in her wistful voice.

"Yes, Mother forgot to send for me when your mother died. One would wonder how she could forget something so important," he said. "But Patience wrote to me."

"But your mother knew by then about your father. She could not have been thinking clearly."

"Yes, of course. I remember now. She told me as I came in the door, then collapsed in my arms. Odd how you forget the worst of things."

"I had been hustled off to my sister Faith in York as soon as fever struck the village. I never got to see my mother again. They said the chance of infection was too great. I wasn't even here for the funeral."

"Losing them changed everything," he said. His spade hit a rock, which he pulled out of his way with his hands. "You expect things to change, but you always think it will be for the better."

"He was very proud of you." Maddie came to stand over the nearly finished hole. Her voice was softer now. "The Saturday before, your father came by with a sack of winter apples for us. Papa locked himself in his study to compose his sermon. Your father looked chilled, and Mother asked me to make him a cup of tea."

Leighton stopped digging and stared at her. He had not mistaken the milkiness of her voice. She was on the point of tears again.

Maddie blinked. "He stayed and talked for a while about his plans for you. He was...happy." She sniffed, compressed her lips, and smiled a watery smile, shutting her tears away.

"Thank you for telling me. Did he say anything about my music?"

She cleared her throat. "Your playing the pianoforte?"

Maddie looked worried, as though the question made her uncomfortable.

"I'm sure he touched on it, along with your talents for farm management and designing buildings."

Leighton grinned. "But he didn't approve of it. He always thought I could spend my time better, though he never said that. I took it that he thought every man was entitled to one vice and playing the pianoforte was not the worst I could have chosen."

"No, it wasn't that way at all."

A stray wisp of hair danced in front of Maddie's right eye, and Leighton thought about how much he loved her, how he had always pictured them together. Why had he waited so long? But he knew why. As long as there was a chance the war would drag him away from her, perhaps permanently, he did not want Maddie's hurt to be greater than his.

A noble thought, but that had given Maddie nothing to look forward to, nothing to hang onto. And if he had been killed, she would never have known how much he loved her.

Chapter Two

Maddie stared at Leighton's worried face touched with doubt, so she came and laid her hand on his shoulder, an automatic attempt to reassure him.

Leighton covered her fingers with his strong, warm hand. "You are cold."

She withdrew her hand, wondering what she had meant by touching him, what he thought of her. "Your father was proud of all your accomplishments. It's just—he was tone deaf. I probably should not tell you that. Now that I recall, I'm sure he asked me not to." She blinked and sniffed but kept her hands under her cloak so he would think it was only the cold making her eyes water.

Leighton leaned his forehead on the shovel handle and chuckled. "All those holiday programs we prepared so laboriously with your papa. My father sat through them and pretended to listen when it must have been agony for him." Leighton shook his head as the laughter took him.

Maddie regarded his close-cropped chestnut hair, so much like his father's, his straight nose and strong chin. She chuckled too, spilling a tear down one cheek, but she did not care now. "He pretended as best he could. Was I wrong to tell you?"

"No, I am glad to know. His tolerance is endearing." Leighton smiled at her. "What do you think? Is this deep enough?"

She glanced at the basket. "He is big for a house cat."

Leighton dutifully dug a little deeper. He wiped the back of his hand across his brow, leaving a smear of dirt behind. Maddie pulled out her handkerchief but restrained herself from cleaning his face. They were no longer children. Why was she so much more conscious of that than Leighton? "That should do it," she said.

"Are you going to say anything?" Leighton asked as he roughly pulled the basket toward him. "I remember that the ceremony for your rabbit went on a good half hour, and we had bouquets of flowers."

Maddie smiled at the memory. "I do not know what would be appropriate for a cat. Perhaps 'Rest in—' "

The basket Leighton was holding suddenly exploded as a ferocious gray striped body screamed and ripped across Leighton's face, knocking him backward onto the mound of dirt.

"Leighton! Good God!" Maddie jumped across the hole and tried to pull his hands away to examine the injury.

"What happened?" Leighton asked, blinking and raising his head groggily. "Who screamed? Are you hurt?"

"Your poor face! It was the cat. He was not dead after all." Maddie used her handkerchief to blot at the welling scratches across his left cheek. Then she saw he had a like set on the right side of his neck and gnawed her lip at her inadequate ministrations.

Leighton stared at her a moment before he went off into a peal of laughter that made it impossible to dab at the scratches. Finally Maddie succumbed to the infection of his mirth and knelt over him, laughing more in relief that he was not seriously injured than in any humor at the situation.

"Be serious, Leighton. You are wounded," she said, grasping him by the cravat and scrutinizing his face. Something happened then. Some unspoken word passed between them and she hesitated as she saw him raise himself enough to kiss her. Not only that, he drew her to his chest as she got lost in her single-minded desire to be close to him. She felt open, in accord with him, as though all the constraint of their many separations had been banished. Moreover, she felt an intense longing for him. Had the effort of keeping away from him created this flood tide of passion? His kiss was hungry and demanding, and she wanted to taste him in return. When she finally drew back, she stared at him in amazement.

"What just happened?" she asked, her lips throbbing and a deep ache of longing growing inside her chest.

"This is what I have been trying to tell you since I met you today." Leighton shook his head and grinned at her. "I love you."

"But Leighton." She pulled back and tried to escape his arms. "You do not fall in love in an instant," she scoffed.

"But I have always loved you. You said it yourself— we are not children anymore. We are perfect together."

"Perfect? We won't be allowed." Maddie struggled in his arms, feeling like a rabbit in a snare, then stilled. It *would* be perfect. As she gazed at Leighton, he raised his head and kissed her again, his lips warm and tender. With her eyes closed like this and his arms around her, she could imagine, for once, being his wife, being with him always.

It was the thing she wanted more than any other future, but would it happen? No matter how much she wanted Leighton, *they* would throw such obstacles in his path that he might give up.

"You are nearly of age," he said, as she lay against his chest. He caressed her cheek with the knuckle of one finger. She raised her head to look at him. He was staring at her with those striking blue eyes that looked as though they were lit from within.

"It isn't just my father we have to deal with. What about your mother?"

"I shall simply tell her we mean to be married. She will see that it is perfect. I need a wife, one who likes music. You have already been performing the duties of Lady Longbridge, so the tenants will accept you. I promise I will be a tolerant husband who does not mind even an occasional comatose cat."

"But Papa will never countenance the match, not in his parish." She sat up and tried to disentangle Leighton's fingers from her long unruly hair.

"He does not own you," Leighton said, helping Maddie as she scrambled to her feet. He heaved himself up and stepped out of the hole, reaching a hand down to pull her up.

"But you don't know what it is like, how he hammers at one for the slightest transgression, even things that are not sins."

"All the more reason to escape him." Leighton embraced her again and kissed her protectively on the forehead this time. She sheltered in his arms and wished she could stay there forever.

"I shall call on your father tomorrow. When will be a good time?"

"I tell you, he has changed since Mother died. He won't like it."

"Why not? He has always had a soft spot for me."

"Only because you have some facility with the keyboard and can transpose music. By some of the things he has said, I take it he has never really trusted you."

"Why not?"

"You are like your father."

"But my father was a good man," he whispered in her ear.

"A nobleman, a man of leisure. 'He toils not, neither does he spin.' "

"But Father toiled a great deal, and so do I. Does your papa think it easy to run an estate, find safe employment for all the men and boys, make sure all the women and children are fed?"

"No, he has no idea. All he knows is that you are in London most of the year. He scarcely stirs from the house."

"I see. You do all his duty visits to the sick. Well, he had better listen to me. I will not have him turning you into a drudge."

"But he needs me to keep house for him," Maddie insisted.

"We shall hire him a housekeeper." Leighton let go of her to gather up the tools. "You will see."

"I still think—oh, the cat."

Leighton glanced through the woods. "What shall we do about it? If he shows up on old Mrs. Horwith's windowsill, he might give her apoplexy."

"No, I think she will merely regard his return from the dead as a miracle. It will be the talk of the village for weeks. Perhaps she will even tell Papa about it and he will preach a sermon on Lazarus."

Leighton laughed and carried the tools back to the shed, where they had tethered Jasper. "You evade my question. When shall I call?"

Maddie handed him his hat and coat. "One time will be as bad as another." She looked toward the church and the rectory cottage with dread, lest her father be watching them.

"I shall come at one o'clock tomorrow, after luncheon but before his nap—take him at his weakest."

"And what will you do when he says no?"

"You are such an alarmist, Maddie. Trust me. He may be a hard man, but he will put your welfare ahead of his own comfort." Leighton kissed her once more before he mounted Jasper.

It felt like the hasty kiss of a soldier leaving to battle some foe. Well, Leighton *was* going home to break the news to his mother. "Shall I tell him why you are calling tomorrow?"

"If you wish. You might put to him the advantage of your marrying the landlord. What a lucky accident that we met today. I thought I would have to wait until Sunday to steal a chance to talk with you alone. It is as though it was meant to be."

Maddie stared after Leighton as he rode off with a wave of his hand.

She waved back numbly. She had not mentioned that he always jumped the hedge in that particular place and that she had seen him riding the fields and had taken that lane to wait for him. She had only wanted to chide him about his neglect of his tenants. She had not meant to kiss him or to awaken all those feelings she had pressed into the back of her heart so carefully, like dried flowers in a book. She had always loved Leighton, even when he was at his most provoking. Talking to him was a joy even when they argued.

Could he be right? Would her father see the advantage of her marriage to his patron? It was true that her father had treated Leighton kindly when he had tutored him as a boy, but something had changed when her mother died. Her father treated everyone badly now. She had been fifteen, well able to take care of the house, but her father had never recovered from that tragedy.

What had happened today was *not* meant to be. She did not believe in divine intervention, not for the good of people. She had only wanted to see Leighton again, to talk to him and satisfy herself that he was well. She had never meant to thrust herself and her problems onto him.

The cat she had not taken into account. She supposed that all the jostling and swinging had revived his aging brain and encouraged him to breathe again. Perhaps there was some force at work here, but she was not sure it was a good one. As for her father countenancing the match, she shook her head as she crossed the cemetery toward the old rectory.

"It would take a miracle."

****

When Maddie dropped her basket and hung up her cloak in the kitchen, she heard her father's footsteps come as far as the open door of his study.

He was in his waistcoat and hooked his thumbs in the armholes as though he had caught her out at something. His springy crop of iron-gray hair made him loom taller than he actually was.

"You are late from your errands. Why do you persist in visiting the poor all the time when you have nothing for them?"

"Someone should check on them." She went to poke up the fire.

Resentment welled up in Maddie, for she always had something for them: food, cloth, medicine. She disliked having to keep Leighton's money a secret, having to spend it slowly so as not to awake suspicions among the tradespeople. She was fortunate to be the one who shopped for her father. He was unlikely to get into casual conversation with the butcher or any of the other local residents. He barely greeted them on Sunday. The only gossip he heard was from the plowmen or the stable hands.

She had managed to dispense Leighton's largesse without detection, and now her mission was over. Leighton was back and there was little for her to do but wait for him. Though she felt relieved, she also felt…what?

Her father was still standing there watching her. "Where were you?"

"I was helping Mrs. Horwith…with her dead cat."

"You have enough work of your own to do at home." He turned to go back to his study. "Is it not time you started dinner?"

"As soon as I get the fire hot. Do you want tea now?"

"Too late. I shall work until dinner."

She followed him into the small room, finding herself clenching her hands together. "Papa, can we afford to hire some help?"

"We have a garden boy. He takes care of the horse. What more help do you need?"

"I mean for the house. It would be good to have someone working here. If I should decide to get married, at least someone would know how you like your meals cooked."

"Who would marry you?" He seated himself behind his desk and looked up at her with a tired shrug.

"Well, there is Leighton."

Vicar Westlake jumped up with such a look of anger on his face that Maddie had no time even to think of cringing. She just stared at him, feeling his look of hatred knife through her.

"I do not want him near you, do you understand?" He pointed at her dramatically as he did when fingering sinners from the pulpit. But she was on to his tricks and would take no guilt that was not her due. Perhaps the cutting look was just another of his theatrics.

"But we were always such friends, and you used to like him. Why shouldn't I marry him?"

"That was before—before I knew what such men are made of. You stay away from Leighton."

"I am almost of age. In a month I can marry whomever I please and you cannot stop me."

"You say one more word about marriage to Leighton and I'll ship you off to your sister's house in Bath."

Maddie could feel the stubborn scowl take possession of her face. "I *will* say another word. Leighton means to call on you tomorrow…about me."

"I see. He means to do the honorable thing and ask for your hand. Well, I shall be waiting for him, but you will not. Go and pack your things."

"Are you serious? What about your dinner?"

"I'll not rest until I've put you beyond his reach." He sat back down at his desk and snatched up a pen.

"But why isn't Leighton acceptable?"

"That is no concern of yours. Now go and pack or I

will take you to the coaching house as you stand."

She knew, by now, any argument would be useless, so she decided to take what action she could. She went to pack her few dresses, disappointed but not surprised. If only there were a way to warn Leighton. He would be rebuffed tomorrow. How could she get word to him about where she was going? For a moment she thought of running away, but it would cause gossip if she appeared at Longbridge Keep with her few possessions tied in a bundle…or even at his sister's house. There was no one else she could shelter with, except perhaps Mrs. Horwith—and then she would have to explain the cat.

Maddie sat on her bed and closed her eyes but did not give in to tears. Odd that she turned weepy only around Leighton. But that was before she knew that he loved her in return. She took a calming breath and straightened her back. His love, now confessed, changed everything.

She had known her father would not approve the marriage. They would have had to go away for the ceremony. She would merely write Leighton from Bath or somewhere along the road. That would work, assuming his mother did not destroy the letter.

That stopped her for a moment, but surely Leighton would remember where her sisters lived, Faith in York and Patience in Bath. Even if he had no word from her, he would figure out where she had gone. And if he did not… She hesitated as she folded a worn jacket and placed it in her valise. If he did not come for her, that would just show that his kiss today had been a whim, that he was not serious about her. Or that he had lost the battle with his mother, though that seemed unlikely. The Leighton she had known six years ago might have lost, but he was different now. She did not know what had happened to him, but she had a feeling he would not be thwarted by something as simple as the disapproval of their parents.

Perhaps this was a test of their love, to see if they were worthy of each other. But that was only in books. In real life there were no grand challenges, only achingly long days of hard work. In her world, things happened for the stupidest reasons, and she might wait forever for Leighton or for word from him. But she had already waited a long time. Her faith was in Leighton.

She pulled a thin sheaf of letters from the back of her washstand drawer. There were only nineteen of them—not much, from all his time away in London. They had usually come with a bank draft after quarter day. Leighton managed to write about London with a wit that was never pretentious. There had been no words of love in them, though she had looked for them. That was why his sudden proposal had surprised her.

She put them carefully in her bag and took from her shelf a small book of household recipes and hints that her mother had written. It was all she had left, all her mother's other things having disappeared with her father's obsessive grief. She flipped it open, but there was no advice appropriate to love torn asunder, just a recipe for strawberry jam.

In this matter she would have to think for herself. She realized the best plan would be to appear to concede to her father's wishes, as she usually did. Once out of his control, she would manage her life as she saw fit and notify him later, if the need arose. She picked up her valise and went downstairs to hitch the horse to the gig.

Chapter Three

Leighton returned Jasper to the care of the single groom at Longbridge and walked down the row of empty stalls to check on Chandros, his new mount, the one Colonel Scoville had given him as a thank-you for all his work during the war in Spain. Chandros flung his gray head up over the stall partition, looking fit and eager to run even after the tiring ride from London. He whinnied to Jasper, and Leighton instructed Nat to stable the two next to each other so they could get acquainted.

Nat was there to take care of the teams of plow horses, the pair of aging carriage horses, and the old hack his sister rode. Leighton shook his head when he recalled the line of beautiful chestnut horses his father had bred. The Earl of Longbridge had cared about his horses almost as much as he did his children, and yet Leighton's mother said he had taken them with him to sell in America and they must have gone down with the ship.

Leighton did not believe her, of course. She had always been jealous of the animals and must have sold them herself after his father left for America. But they had been gone by the time he came home and there was no point in quarreling over it after they found out his father had died as well.

It hurt that his father had not told him of his plans ahead of time. The brief note Cook had handed him, instructing him to take care of the estate, seemed an inadequate farewell and was the first Leighton had heard about the uncle or the plantation in America. Leighton suspected the trip had more to do with getting away from Mother than visiting a brother.

He stroked Chandros' nose. This half-Andalusian, with his short back and sturdy legs, held some promise as a stud. If Leighton got some likely mares, he and Maddie would have a stable full of riding horses in a few years.

Maddie riding with him and the girls ended with his father's death. He was looking forward to telling his sisters Amy and Susan the news of his betrothal. Less so his mother, but she would get used to the idea. Once she had seemed quite fond of Maddie.

Leighton walked toward the house, glancing around the walled stone courtyard. The square tower that formed the center of the sprawling house had been a fortified keep in medieval times, and now everything looked cold and unwelcoming, not the place he would like to bring Maddie to live.

He shook his head as he approached the back door and cast a worried glance at the chimney and coping stones. He had ordered them worked on last time he'd been home, but his mother had countermanded that order, like so many others. How would they get along, now that he meant to stay?

The house sounded empty as his footsteps echoed down the dark hall to the great room. The stone walls and ancient arms hanging above head height were softened by new curtains at the windows and some chairs he did not remember from before. His pianoforte was still in the same corner. It would have sounded better in a wood-lined room, but he had no heart to move it.

He sat down and touched a single key, drawing forth a melancholy note to die in the chilly air. Would he and Maddie come to the place that they could not stand each other, as his parents had done? Impossible. He and Maddie had so much in common, whereas his parents had shared nothing. Idly, he wondered why his father had ever married his mother.

He began to play from memory. Maddie and the resurrected cat made him smile, but that made the scratches on his face hurt. Maddie was different, a practical woman who never let pride get in the way of doing what was right. But there was a thread of wildness in her that escaped at the most surprising moments, like one lock of her glorious brown hair getting loose from under her cloak and hinting at the hidden passions within.

Leighton was still lost in the music and thoughts of Maddie when he realized that coming toward him down the long hall was the sound of an argument between his mother and his younger sister Susan. He resisted the urge to rush to the end of the work so they could not spoil it. He played louder to drown out their dispute over ribbons and yard goods. Consequently, the piece ended with a pounding flourish rather than a modest trill. He thought he liked it better that way, as though he was having the last word.

"Leighton, Mother is making me wear ugly dresses," Susan complained.

He turned to look at her and noticed her face was still red from crying.

"Nothing could look ugly on you."

"But white?" she complained. She held out the sides of the skirt in disgust. "I look like a giant strawberry perched on a table napkin."

Leighton shook his head to rid it of this image but found himself agreeing as he regarded her in the muslin creation. Where his father had passed on to him and his older sister a crisp russet crop of hair, the color had come out in Susan as a startling and unlikely red.

"Perhaps you could wear a cream-colored shawl."

"See, Mother, Leighton agrees with me."

"Leighton knows nothing about it."

Lady Longbridge threw herself down in one of the new chairs and was regarding her children critically. She wore a light blue gown today, and her own blonde hair was impeccably dressed. Leighton realized that a stranger would never think her their mother.

"And where did you get those scratches on your face?"

He winced. "An encounter with an angry cat."

"May I go to London to shop?" his sister begged.

"Yes, of course, but what would that solve?" Leighton asked. "Mother would have to go with you."

"But she would see what the other girls are wearing. And I could make my come-out next year in style rather than in these provincial rags." Susan again held her skirt out dramatically.

Leighton traded uncomfortable looks with his mother.

"Rags? I'll have you know I gave two guineas for the goods for that dress."

"Well, you wasted—"

"I have an idea," Leighton said. "Why not ask Amy if she wants to go with you to London?"

"Amy has no taste," his mother snapped. "Look who she married."

"She married Ross Hemmings, the squire's son and a good friend. By the way, Amy and Ross are dining with us tonight."

"You are just trying to get rid of me," his mother snapped. "I suppose you are too busy to come to London with us yourself."

"The planting is done and the early hay in—thanks to Ross overseeing our people, I might add. But there is years' worth of work to be done on the house, things that have been put off." He glared at her.

"You should have been here, rather than socializing in London. Much good it did. You never brought a single eligible man home for your sisters, never an invitation anywhere. I suppose it's not respectable for us to stay in your lodgings in London."

"I let those go. Tibbs is packing up my things and bringing them home. You can stay at a hotel when you go to London."

"Your father would never keep a house in London either. So we are shut out of society in this backwater." She glared around the expensively decorated great room.

"This was a backwater before you married him," Leighton reminded her. "Are we agreed? You stay at a hotel for this visit, and we will hire a house next year for Susan's come-out."

"And after that?" His mother looked a challenge at him. "I thought the whole purpose of your long stays in town was to find a wife. Have you given up?"

"No, I have indeed asked someone to marry me."

"Really?" His mother sat up straight. "Well, why didn't you tell me? She will expect a house in town. Who is she?"

"I do not think she cares at all about London. I have

asked Maddie to marry me."

There was dead silence in the room as his mother gaped at him. "Constance Madeline Westlake? The parson's daughter?" His mother's outrage pulled her from the chair to her feet.

"You know she prefers to be called Maddie. I find that I—"

"Are you insane?" she demanded as she launched herself across the room, all signs of fatigue gone. "Are *all* my children going to flout my wishes?"

Susan gave a resigned sigh and plopped down on the piano bench with Leighton as their mother paced the room.

"Why not Maddie?" Leighton asked. "She is already well-acquainted with all our people and the duties of Lady Longbridge, since she has been performing them these last six years."

"She is an encroaching dowd. She has managed to convince you she deserves to take my place just by visiting the poor and acting the grand lady."

Susan looked up at her mother. "Maddie has not the money to dress well."

Their mother stopped in front of them with her hands on her hips. "Well, she has one thing, I grant her— more brains than either of you. She has Leighton ready to marry her because he feels sorry for her and guilty for neglecting his tenants. Just think about this while you are having this sudden attack of conscience. How about sparing a thought for us, your family, whom you have equally neglected ever since you left school?"

"I came home in the winters."

"Oh, yes, when you are needed the least. Meantime, I have had all the decisions put on me."

Leighton stood up. "I admit that I have neglected my family and my tenants. It's a poor landlord who feeds them punch and cake once a year when they need meat every week, but the managing of the estate is what I pay Ross to do. And it would be a damned sight easier for him if you did not cross him at every turn."

"I should have some say about what happens in my own home."

"All you ever do is obstruct." Leighton raised his hands in exasperation as though he were about to conduct a group of players, but Susan's doleful face caught his eye.

His sister sniffed. "Please stop arguing. I cannot bear it. It's just like when Father was here."

"I have the headache," their mother announced, as though there was only one headache in the world and she had it. "If I am supposed to be cordial to the guests *you* invited into *my* house tonight, I am going to have to rest." She swept out of the room, and Leighton shrugged and turned to his sister.

"What about it? Will you be able to tolerate Mother in London for a week or so?"

"I had rather you were taking me."

He shook his head as he pulled at the bow on her sleeve. "What do I know of ribbons and laces?"

"It's not that. You would be on my side."

"I just came back from London. The whole town has run mad with the peace celebrations. And Ross does deserve a rest."

"Very well. If Amy and Ross are going, I can manage Mother." She stood up and smoothed the hated dress down. "Leighton?"

"Yes?"

"I don't remember Father very well, but you are like him. That much I know."

"I argue with Mother as frequently, at any rate."

"She is not a happy person. We should accept that. But is she right about Maddie?"

"You are not a snob. I thought you liked Maddie."

"Of course I do. I mean, are you marrying her because you feel sorry for her?"

Leighton thought for a moment and shook his head with a sad smile. "No, because I feel sorry for me."

****

When Ross and Amy arrived for dinner, Leighton had to answer a gantlet of questions about the scratches on his face. Neither of them swallowed the cat story, and he was amazed that the truth seemed so unlikely to them. After all, they knew Maddie as well as he did.

His mother, as it turned out, was too fatigued to join them for dinner, so the four of them could speak freely about farm matters, the repairs to the house that Lady Longbridge had circumvented, or anything else they chose. Even so, they were halfway through the meal before Leighton brought up his plan for the trip to London. Ross seemed agreeable to let Amy go, but she was reluctant to leave him when there was so much to be done in the summer. And she did not want to try to manage their two children herself, nor to leave them at home.

"Very well." Ross's dark eyes glittered from the wine they had broached for the meal. "I will escort you to the city and get you settled with enough help to keep track of Jules and Robert. If it looks as though you do not need me, I'll slip back here. You send for me when you want to come home."

"I wish we could all go," Amy said. "But someone has to watch over the work here."

"Leighton is going to offer for Maddie," Susan said, then glanced at her brother. "Or wasn't I supposed to tell?"

He grinned. "Of course you may tell Ross and Amy. Just do not shout it from the housetop until the date is firm."

"Congratulations," Ross said, rising to shake Leighton's hand. "I always thought you two would make a match of it. You were always at loggerheads when alone, but back to back in any fight."

"I suppose marriage will not change that," Leighton said with a chuckle.

Amy smiled at him. "I feel happy that Maddie will finally escape her morose father. We all mourn, but his wife has been gone six years and he is still taking it out on Maddie."

"Perhaps it is harder for him to accept, being a man of God," Ross guessed.

"That is no reason for him to be such a tyrant," Amy returned.

"Well, I still have to face the tyrant at one o'clock tomorrow, so wish me luck."

The girls left Leighton and Ross to their glasses of port, and Susan promised Amy the ugly white dress if it fit her.

Leighton turned to his longtime friend, remembering fishing and riding together while knowing they would someday have charge of their adjoining estates. "Do you mind so much taking them to the city? Ordinarily I would not worry, but the populace can be unruly in its celebrations. Besides, you could use a holiday yourself."

Ross leaned back in his chair. "I do not mind the country, but I like to see my Amy smile."

"How are the children?"

"Right as rain. They could use some neighbors to play with. I am pleased about you and Maddie. I have worried about her. Some say old Westlake isn't sane."

Leighton took a sip of the pungent wine and swirled the remainder in his glass. "His sermons are the most severe I have ever heard, as though he is angry at the world."

"Puts me in mind of your mother. I cannot say two words to her without putting her in a temper."

"Oh, and I thought it was only me. I take it the coping stones are still loose and the chimneys still need to be cleaned?"

"Aye." Ross sighed heavily. "I hired the men in Hereford and had to pay them a day's wage when she had them turned away at the door."

"I'll have them here and done while you are still in London."

"I'll give you their direction. She'll be fit to be tied, you making dust all over the house."

"I see the new bridge has not progressed, either."

"I got the oaks felled and the tenants, both yours and mine, were desperate glad to get the firewood from the limbs, but when your mother got wind of our plans she pitched a fit. We had some dry weather for plowing then, so I let the beams rest where we felled them."

Ross stared into the fireplace as though he was seeing the felling of the trees again. Every estate kept an oak grove for building beams and repairs. Last Christmas he and Ross had chosen the ones to make the beams for the bridge.

"It would have been better if they had been skidded into place during the winter," Leighton mused, "but I'll have a look at them. It's downhill to the river. We might get them down there. If I can construct a crane, we can winch them into place."

"You've got the head for that sort of thing. The planking has been sawn and is drying in the upper story of the barn. I had the men sneak it in there."

"I saw it. Good work. If the weather stays clear, we might be able to manage the new bridge in a week."

"That would be capital. I shiver every time someone drives a loaded wagon over that old heap of stone."

"It is not safe. I do not know why Mother persists in thinking it will last forever."

"She never let your father get this far. If you get the bridge built, you're a better man than any of us."

"And if I get the chimneys cleaned, I might be able to have a fire in my room without suffocating in the smoke."

Ross laughed, then got a serious look on his face. "Are you ever going to tell her what you really did when you were supposed to be in London?"

"No." Leighton emptied his glass and stared at the decanter of port shining darkly red in the candlelight like a beaker of blood. "No one around here knows except you. I think my secret is safe."

Chapter Four

The next day, Leighton regretted putting off the interview with Maddie's father until the afternoon. He finished reviewing the accounts from Ross, well satisfied that the profit from the estate was not at the expense of his tenants. Besides, most of his income was from investments. There would be plenty to bring his sister out in style and to provide for her dowry, which was more important.

He then spent an hour pacing the library, rehearsing his speech and answers to all the arguments Westlake might think of against the match.

After a large luncheon, the shopping expedition left for London, all of them smiling except his mother, who looked about the courtyard as though she were seeing it for the last time.

Leighton went back inside to get his riding crop and paused to straighten his neckcloth in the hall mirror, painfully aware of his marked face. He supposed he would have to answer the vicar's silly questions about the scratches, too.

Nat had driven the family to Hereford in the ancient traveling carriage. The party would change horses there and the groom would be home by nightfall. Leighton went to the stable and saddled Chandros himself.

As he rode to the vicarage, he owned to being more nervous than he had let on to Maddie. He tethered his horse in the orchard and walked up the back way to the kitchen door, past the blooming mock-orange bush, which exuded an enticing hint of orange perfume and made the whole garden sweet and fresh.

At the last moment, he realized this more formal occasion might call for his entrance through the front parlor. He walked around the house toward the front, admiring Maddie's rosebushes and morning glories as they infringed on the bench under the front window. How often he had lounged on that bench, scratching out some bars of music on a slate or doing a Latin lesson while Maddie and Patience peeled apples, picked flowers, or played tag in the front garden. He should have known he loved Maddie even then.

Leighton's knock went unanswered for some minutes, and he pictured his beloved trying to tidy her wanton brown ringlets, smooth her sober dress, or look as if she did not care about the outcome of this interview when actually she loved him just as much. He was sure of it.

When the door opened, it was not Maddie who let Leighton in but Westlake himself, wearing his professional scowl. As he followed the man into the small dusty-smelling study, Leighton wiped the foolish grin from his face. Perhaps this would not be as easy as he had assured Maddie it would.

Leighton knew his worth down to the farthing and was prepared to negotiate when his request for Maddie's hand produced reserve. What he was not prepared for was a flat, emphatic, "No!" from the man behind the desk.

"You cannot have understood me, sir. I wish to marry Maddie. What makes you speak as though I suggest some misalliance?"

"You have corrupted my daughter, sir. Yesterday she was content to her duties."

"Duties? To care for your house?" Leighton gestured around him. "But how can that compare to her duty to marry? Her sisters have done so."

"Against my wishes. Well, I tell you, sir, I have but one daughter left and she will not desert me."

"But we will be living scarcely twenty minutes away," Leighton insisted.

"I tell you, I won't have it, sir."

"I would prefer to marry with your permission, but if you deny it, I am prepared to proceed without it."

"You will never see her again. I forbid it."

"I will see her at church, if nowhere else," Leighton argued.

"That you shall not. I knew who I was dealing with." Westlake rose from his chair and folded his arms with finality. "You are willful, just like your father. I have sent her away, sir, and she will stay gone until you are safely wedded to another."

"Sent her away? But that is insane. You have lost her even more surely than when she marries me and lives next door."

"Nevertheless, that is what I have done. You'll not have access to her and will soon grow tired of waiting. Your kind always does."

Leighton studied the pale face, intense with hatred. "You—you haven't hurt her?"

"I have put her beyond your reach."

For a moment Leighton had some notion that Westlake had murdered Maddie. The very thought stunned him, but he pushed it aside. The man might be mad, but that did not make him a murderer. "But why? Why am I not acceptable?"

"You come here with that face and have the gall to ask me that question?" Westlake reached out and grasped Leighton's chin in his hand to better scrutinize the marks. Leighton jerked his head away.

"It was a cat, old Mrs. Horwith's cat."

"The one that died yesterday? A likely story!"

"But it is the truth. He is not dead."

"Out!"

Leighton left and walked back around the house with the summer flowers nodding in the breeze, mocking his unhappiness. His worst day in Spain he had never felt as incompetent as this. He glanced up at Maddie's window and felt empty. If she was in the house, she would give him some sign. Had her father actually done her some harm?

The mock-orange bush outside the back door was so laden with fragrant flowers the limbs curved down to the ground. He could remember retreating under there with Maddie when his father had given him some puzzle to solve. She had been a great help to him, and he had sorely missed her advice all these years. Usually Mrs. Westlake would bring them fresh gingerbread and milk. How could such a warm and loving person have married such a cold man? And how could Leighton win him over?

It was simple. He could not. When he found Maddie, he would just have to convince her of that. He met the garden boy near the tool shed, but the lad only gawked at Leighton's questions about where Maddie had gone.

Then he rode into Longton village and discovered that the vicar's gig had delivered Maddie to the single inn the previous afternoon, where Westlake had hired a groom to drive her to Hereford. There she might take the stage for Worcester, Tewkesbury, Gloucester or any number of other places. But the vicar had driven her only as far as the village and not stayed. Even if he hired someone to escort her the rest of the journey, surely she could have evaded them, if not before Hereford, then at least there.

On the surface, it seemed a simple matter to Leighton. *He* would have rented a horse and ridden back to Longbridge Keep. But Maddie was a woman and one who had probably spent every bit of money he had given her in feeding the poor. She might have no real choice but to go where her father sent her. Leighton's task was to discover where that was. It should not be a difficult puzzle. At least she was alive and she knew he loved her. If it took the rest of his life, he would find her.

He rode home through a drenching rain and hardly noticed it except that he found himself comparing it to the day Maddie's mother had been buried. Westlake had presided, but with little to say, and no one had remarked it. He had just lost his wife.

Westlake's coldness to him could no longer be ignored or put down to the grief of a widower. He was contemptuous of the whole Stone family, even though he derived his living from them. Leighton would not take that away, for revenge was not in his style. Besides, he would marry Maddie wherever he found her, and Westlake would have to accept him, like it or not.

****

Maddie looked out the window of the coach, straining to see if Leighton might be coming yet. She had stayed the night in Hereford at the same inn as the old ostler who was in charge of her trip. She had written a quick note to Leighton and given it to the innkeeper to post, but the ostler had caught her at it. Probably he told the innkeeper they were trying to prevent an elopement, so she wouldn't give much for Leighton's chances of getting the letter. She could have escaped the inn but could never have walked the whole way to Longbridge Keep. She had considered it, but she might have missed Leighton if he came across country. Besides, she still hated the idea of begging for refuge.

The ostler had bought her ticket this morning and waited to put her on the stage to Gloucester. At the last minute he had put a few coins into her hand, possibly enough to feed her until she got to her sister's house in Bath but not enough to get back to Leighton.

The steps were put up, the door closed, and the team started forward, slamming her against the seat. She felt powerless to stop what was happening to her, and she hated that. Whatever the outcome, she would never let her father have control of her again. If he ever wrote Patience that she was to come home again, she would refuse. If he came to wrest her away, she would leave. By then she would have been able to communicate with Leighton or find a position for herself.

She realized with a start that she had already doubted Leighton, that she did not absolutely believe he would find her. She pondered for a time if it was worse to know that he loved her and then have that snatched away, rather than never to know. She had to agree with the storybooks on this one. His declaration of love, however incongruously delivered in a grave, was precious to her, and she had to nurture it and not lose hope.

If he had started out after her at one o'clock

yesterday, he could not possibly be to Hereford by now, not if he rode his horse to death. And she certainly did not want that. Perhaps he would overtake her at Gloucester.

****

The downpour through that day and the next gave Leighton plenty of time to pace the study and speculate on where Maddie had been sent. He couldn't take either of his beasts out in this weather, though he had ridden in such drenchings often enough in the Peninsula. Maddie had a sister near York and one in Bath. It would make more sense if the vicar had sent her to York, since Faith lived in the country and might be hard to locate, but Bath was no more than two days ride. It would be foolish not to see if she was staying with Patience. As soon as Ross returned to take care of things and the weather cleared, he would saddle Chandros and follow her.

Then it hit him that he had seen Nat ride out on his sister's hack just after Amy and Ross had arrived for dinner that first night. Had his Mother sent a note to warn Westlake that Leighton meant to call? Perhaps she had more to do with the blatant refusal than the vicar. Most such men would have been glad to see a daughter so well married. It would be something to task his mother with when she blew up over him getting the chimneys cleaned.

Leighton hit his fist on the desk. Would it never stop raining? He could ride as far as Hereford and take a coach to Bath, but he hated to leave the place unattended. With Ross gone and the weather so uncertain, anything might happen to the tenants, and someone had to be here to make decisions.

Over the next few days, the downpour turned the

fields into quagmires and the roads into torture traps. They had gotten all the herds and flocks under shelter and were feeding them the remains of last year's hay. The sheep had already been shorn, but if they couldn't get them dry, they would have wool maggot, hoof rot, or some equally disgusting malady among them. The men were hugging the firesides, not looking forward to replanting what the wretched weather was rotting in the field, when the boy set to watch the river brought word that the stone bridge had washed away.

Leighton had Chandros saddled. Instead of the romp the horse was expecting, Leighton rode him to the river in the early dawn to assess the damage. He would have to lay a new bridge, and speedily. There would be no getting to or from the village until the work was done. At least he did not have to prepare a new site. The stone pillars on either bank were sound. It was the one in the middle that had given way.

He decided they would have to construct the crane on the other bank while all the teams that could be mustered dragged the beams into place. But to get material across in this flood, someone would have to cross with the first rope.

The next day the wood and ropes for the crane had been dragged to the bank. It was still misting but not so badly that they could not work in it. The men urged him to ride across, but he would not risk Chandros or Jasper in such a current. Even if Leighton was swept downstream during his swim, he would have the end of the rope. So he took off his boots, stripped to his breaches, tied the rope about himself, and leaped out, grateful for all the swimming practice as a boy.

He had been prepared for a strong current, but this

one caught him and had him at its mercy. As he had calculated, the sweep of the river around the bend drove him against the other bank and he was only a hundred yards downstream when he climbed out. A cheer went up, and he felt grander than he ever had in the Peninsula. At least this was constructive work.

He oversaw operations himself. After pulling across a block-and-tackle, he was able to winch over a boat with three men. Then they pulled across the wood for the crane, and he started them on the assembly of that as he oversaw the dragging of the beams to the river with all those attendant difficulties. Both tasks took days because of the rain and unexpected cold.

Each night they had to make their work secure and get everyone back across. He fed them in the large kitchen at the keep, where they dried their clothes before carrying provisions home for their families. He had to admit he enjoyed the camaraderie, but he would have relished this first big project more if only he was not so worried about Maddie.

The rain let up after a week, but the river ran high another day and a half as he tested and improved the crane. With the beams parked at the edge of the bank, the workers began winching the end of the first one across. When its weight levered off the opposite bank, it looked as if it would slide into the raging torrent, but the crane held and they winched the end across and into place as slick as you please. They all believed it was a happy accident until the second one slipped into place just as easily. Then they cheered. But they set to work again and nailed the braces and planking into place. The work went faster now, even though the rain returned intermittently.

Leighton had dispatched one express to Ross, now

begging him to keep the ladies in town as long as possible since there would be no way to get them home without a long detour on very bad roads. There was every chance that some other bridge or ford would be impassible and they could not make it at all.

In his mind, he kept going over Maddie's possible route. It had only just started to rain when she left, so if she was bound for Bath she should have been safe enough, but possibly not if she was traveling the whole way to York.

Then it occurred to him he should have sent a lad into the village, even if he had to walk, to see if Maddie had sent a letter. Well, in another day he could go himself. But why hadn't he put her first? Possibly because he was a man of duty, and he knew she would understand since she was a creature of duty herself. Still, he should have thought of it, even though he was so tired each night he was asleep as soon as he stretched out in bed.

Chapter Five

It was nearly dark and the men were dumping the last loads of gravel and stone for the new approaches to the bridge when the Longbridge carriage, pulled by job horses, came into sight.

His mother leaned out the window to assess the situation and shouted for Leighton to get inside before he caught his death. He shook his head "no" and rode ahead of them toward the house. He had to tell Cook the men would be coming in early to eat, and he wanted her to get the servants to bundle up extra food for them. Besides, he had to get their pay ready for them. They had more than earned it.

Only Susan and his mother were in the coach, which meant they had left Ross's family at their home. How like his mother to ignore flood and devastation, to have no word of admiration for their quite remarkable feat, but to worry about him catching cold. Well, he would probably satisfy her on that score, for he had inhaled a bit of water in his swim and had not been able to get his lungs clear this whole week.

Worst of all, he had not been able to pursue Maddie. What if her coach had broken down? She could have been stranded anywhere in this weather. He had put his duty to Longbridge ahead of her welfare, just as he had always put his war duties ahead of her. If she had reached Bath safely, surely she would have sent him word. Of course, with the bridge out, no mail could have come until today. But he would find out tomorrow when he rode to the village.

"Soaked to the skin!" his mother chanted as she invaded Leighton's bedroom later. "Malcolm, how could you allow this?"

"He's your butler, Mother," Leighton croaked, "not my keeper."

"And well you have need of a keeper. More hot water, Malcolm, and be quick about it. Someone start a fire."

"I am a grown man," Leighton said nasally, then coughed. "And I want no fire in this room. The smoke will kill me."

"With as little sense as a boy. Do you not recall how subject you are to inflammation of the lungs?"

"Vividly," Leighton replied, toweling his hair dry, "but I have not had a single case of it since I left home."

"You may have killed yourself over a stupid bridge. All so that we could get home again." His mother then burst into tears, and Leighton regretted arguing with her. He embraced her even though he was getting her terribly wet.

"Were the roads very bad?"

"Very." She looked up at him with tired, reddened eyes, clutching the damp lapels of his coat. "We should have stayed in London, but I was worried about you, what you might be doing, and I was right to worry. You were engaged in just such stupid behavior as will be your death."

"Someone had to manage the construction."

"Someone else could have."

"Actually, no." Leighton released her and smiled

into her worried face, glad that she cared so much about him, even if she had an odd way of showing it. "These men are willing and courageous, but they have not the knowledge to plan such a project. We worked well together. Did you see how proud they were to have finished just in time for you to drive across it?"

"Yes, I saw. But it will cost you dear."

"You seem to forget. I spent years away at school in unheated rooms without taking the slightest harm, not so much as a sniffle. I almost never needed a fire in my London lodgings, and when I was in—"

She looked at him expectantly, but he could not tell her, not while she was this distraught.

"I do not believe you, Leighton. I think you almost died many times these past years and are too stubborn to tell me."

He forced a smile to his face. "You worry about me too much. Now go and see to your baggage. I am sure you have bought ells of material, and if it has got wet, you will have to dry it."

"Don't you realize how important you are?"

Leighton laughed and stripped off his wet coat. "In the great scheme of things, I am not that important."

"Nothing must happen to you."

Leighton hesitated, then began to unbutton his wet shirt. "Why not?"

"If you die, we lose Longbridge Keep. It goes to some relative we do not even know."

Leighton felt his jaw clench, a shiver running through him that had nothing to do with his illness. "Yes. How could I have forgotten that. Much does depend on me."

She did go away then, without even realizing how

she had hurt him. He could feel the fever mounting as he changed into dry clothes, then went to the kitchen to count out the money for his work crew. He overpaid all of them, for not one had let him down. Then he told them to report to Ross on the morrow, since he himself had a trip to make. He tried not to cough, not to let them see his weakness, and they left after their meal, happy and victorious. He needed sleep more than anything, so he crawled up to bed.

His mother returned later to add another coverlet to the pile that seemed to be crushing Leighton's chest. When she woke him, he discovered Malcolm had started a smoky fire in the fireplace even though Leighton told him not to. He drank the tea they gave him but knew it was doing no good. He had spent many a night as a boy sitting up sleeping to try to keep his lungs clear, and he did not look forward to the experience.

As soon as his mother and Malcom left him alone, he escaped the laden bed and flung open the window for some cool air. This, of course, made the fireplace in his room smoke even more now that it could finally draw through the window, so he put on his robe and made his way to the kitchen. Cook was sitting up, as he knew she would be.

"What do you want to try? Horehound or mint?" she asked as she went to the fireplace.

"Mix them and make it strong, Cook. I'll need all the help I can get to fight this off."

"They never listen to you," she said as she picked up the kettle of hot water with the tail of her apron. "I have some licorice root here, as well." She poured boiling water into the teapot and Leighton thought he could smell the mint brewing already.

"And I never listen to them. It's a fair exchange, I suppose." Leighton coughed from deep in his chest and sat at the large kitchen table.

"I've warned them about the chimneys, but your mother won't have them cleaned. 'Too much dust,' she says in the spring. Then in the fall, it's 'we'll wait until spring.'"

"I'll see to it…when I can. You did great work yourself, cooking for so many these past days."

"It was a joy seeing them all work together. You have a way with people. Your father had it and so do you. That's one thing your mother cannot take from you."

"Cook?"

"Aye?"

"You've known Vicar Westlake all his life."

"Aye. I'll not say aught against a man of the cloth." She swirled a spoon through the tea and sniffed it before pouring it through a strainer into a pewter tankard.

Leighton watched her attentively. "He used to seem a good sort, but have you ever doubted his reason?"

"He may pass as a vicar, but as a man—he was like a dog over a bone with his poor wife and treated the girls little better. The man would be more suited to be a jailer."

"Why did no one ever tell me?"

"Not my place. Here's your tea. I've added a dollop of brandy to it for taste."

"Thank you, Cook. You are a life saver." Leighton took a tentative sip, but the brandy had cooled it so that it was drinkable. He took a long slow swallow, feeling some immediate relief in his throat. "I offered for Maddie and he refused me. Why?"

The old woman froze, the hitch in her usually graceful movements apparent to even the feverish

Leighton. Now why would that surprise her?

"Constance Madeline. A good girl, that one. Always out and looking after the old and sick. Many's the time she has come to me for herbs. And never a thought for herself."

"You are evading the question. Why would he refuse me?"

The old woman swallowed and sat on the bench beside him. "There was bad blood between him and your father. He wants nothing to do with the Stones, and I wager he resents drawing his living from you."

"But why? What could Father have done to him?"

"That I cannot say."

Leighton stared at her. It was the one time she did not look him in the eye.

He took another slow sip of tea and felt some strength coming back into him. But perhaps it was only the brandy. "Could Vicar Westlake have...murdered his wife?"

Cook jumped and glared at him. "What the devil brought that on?"

"Maddie was never allowed to see her."

"Mrs. Westlake died of the fever. Now drink that before you pass off the same route." She jumped up to bring him pillows and a blanket.

Leighton had several coughing fits during the night, as he slept at the table in the kitchen, leaning on a pillow. But he survived it with Cook several times changing the aromatic poultice that seemed to penetrate from his chest to his backbone. By morning, he felt like living and more than ever like finding Maddie.

His appearance at the breakfast table would have been enough to throw the rest of the household into fidgets and admonishments to get back to bed. But his announcement that he meant to leave for a week had his sister and mother talking at once in their attempts to dissuade him. He calmly drank his coffee and ate his meal, amazed that he was now able to tune them out so effectively. Perhaps his ears were just stuffed.

When Malcolm ignored Leighton's instructions to pack his gear, Leighton began the job. He was used to looking out for himself now. He even carried the valises to the stable and, when Nat seemed reluctant to obey him, began saddling Chandros himself. He saddled Jasper, too, so he could use him as a pack animal. It would be like an expedition into Spain. Finally, he led the horses out into the courtyard and mounted.

He saw Susan disappear from the hall window. His mother ran out of the house before he had gotten to the gate.

"But where are you going in this condition?" she demanded, dropping her shawl and wringing her hands. Susan followed her out of the house and helplessly picked up the garment.

He thought about telling her the truth but decided against it. "To get myself better."

"But you can recover here, where we can take care of you."

"If you smother me with quilts and a smoking fireplace, that is not likely to happen soon. The cold leaves much sooner if I move about and breathe clean air."

"You know nothing about it. Now stop this nonsense and get back to bed."

Cook came shuffling out in her broken shoes and handed him a tin of herbs and a flask of hot tea. He thanked her for his life—again—and waved goodbye to his mother and sister.

"But where are you going?" Susan called. "To London?"

He smiled and shook his head as he waved to her. He felt a wonderful lightness about him, but that might be the fever working. He was going on a quest to find Maddie, and the less he said about that in front of his mother the better.

"But when will you be back?" his mother shouted.

"As soon as you have the chimneys cleaned." That would hold her for a good long while.

He trotted the horses down the drive with a sigh of relief. He had escaped. Why had that been so hard to accomplish? Because he had far rather stay at Longbridge, which he loved. But not with his mother thwarting him at every turn. He would have been better off leaving the bridge work for drier weather. But he was a creature of duty and knew he had to finish the bridge or feel the guilt of it. To hell with duty now. He would let nothing else get in the way of finding his future wife.

Chapter Six

Maddie stared across at her eldest sister, a respectable widow now and something of a personage in Bath. Patience Carter sat at the breakfast table having her first tea of the day at nine in the morning, whereas Maddie had been up at seven, walked the dog in the garden, read several chapters of a boring novel, and started a letter.

She crumbled her muffin on her plate and, catching the lap dog's eager movement out of the corner of her eye, coyly dropped a chunk of it on the carpet.

Patience looked up from her newspaper, regarding her sister over her pince-nez.

"Guess what I saw on our walk," Maddie demanded to distract her from the dog.

"I cannot imagine. Did you stay in the garden as I asked?"

"Yes, of course, though it is a small garden. I saw a man in a purple coat."

"Purple or lavender?"

"It makes no odds. He was still absurd."

"Was he using a walking stick and leading a little pug?"

"Yes, do you know him?"

"He's one of Bath's oddities. We have many. In fact you can be as eccentric as you like here and people will just accept it. *You* should fit right in."

"I am an oddity, then," Maddie concluded. "I always suspected as much."

"Don't change. Be yourself. You will be a novelty. So long as you dress in good taste and do not obviously flout any conventions, you will be accepted for my sake."

"But why can't I go for a walk in the town? One of the maids could come with me."

"Not until we have you attired in one of the dresses being made for you. Then I shall take you to the Pump Room. We are going to have such fun this season, Maddie."

"If you say so." Maddie did not care about the new dresses that were being sewn or the Pump Room. Leighton had not come for her, had not even tried to contact her by mail. So he did not care after all. And when that became obvious to her father, he would send for her and expect her to come back to the vicarage.

"We'll visit my dressmaker this morning, and with any luck, make your debut at the Pump Room this afternoon."

"But why go to the Pump Room? You said the water is foul."

"To be seen. I know Papa asked me to find you a situation, but there is no need. I have plenty of money. With your looks, we can find you a husband, instead."

"But I do not want a husband."

Patience threw the newspaper aside. "Why did he send you to me? You have not done anything to disgrace yourself?"

"What did he say in his letter?"

"That you were about to make a misalliance. Who is he, Maddie? Not the plowman."

"No. Leighton Stone asked me to marry him."

Patience sat back and nervously looked out the window. "Leighton, the Earl of Longbridge."

"Yes, of course. You know Leighton. He is not stuffy and never acts like he considers himself better than one of us."

"But, you see, Papa dislikes the whole family. Believe me, it is better that I find someone else for you."

"I suppose it does not matter. Leighton cannot really have been interested." She pressed her lips together and fought back the tears. It got easier every time she managed it.

Patience reached across and patted her hand. "Go, get your shawl. A new dress will fix that frown."

Maddie turned and trudged from the room. No point in telling Patience how she felt and none at all in dragging her generous sister down into her black mood with her. But after the rejection by Leighton, whom she loved, she was not about to get entangled with any other man.

Maddie had been in Bath almost two weeks and Leighton had not written to her. The thought that *all* her letters, at least three a week, had been misdirected was hard to swallow. She had expected too much of him. His mother had prevailed after all.

By his own admission, Leighton had been little more than a clerk in London, however intrepid he'd been as a boy. She had found it hard to write those letters to him from Bath, including the one that lay unfinished in her room, for they all sounded so needy. And she was tired of being the needy one, tired of taking his money and dispensing it to his dependents. She wanted to do something for herself.

Staying at the vicarage had been hard, but at least she had been useful. Here there was nothing for her to do except walk the dog, read books from the circulating library, or relay her sister's orders to the servants. She felt bored and worthless. She worried in odd moments about Mrs. Horwith and the others.

She tried not to think about Leighton at all, for if she did, she cried into her tea in a distressing way. He was not coming, and that was that. So she would make a new life for herself, but she would never go back to the vicarage. On that she was determined. If not for the interference of her father, she would have married Leighton and never had to know how weak-willed he was. As for his mother, Maddie knew she would have had no problem dealing with her. She handled difficult people all the time.

****

Leighton left Chandros and Jasper at the hotel stable in the hands of an admiring and competent groom. He had chosen Prad's Hotel, even though it was out of the way near the river, because it did have a stable. Besides, the walk to and from the center of town would do him good.

He was about to shoulder his valises when the head lad snapped his fingers and motioned for an ostler to carry his bags around front. As Leighton expected, they did have a room for him. Had he not had a coughing fit in the lobby, Leighton might have been unable to convince the desk clerk that such a strapping young man as himself had come to Bath for his health. He wrote out a request to his man Tibbs in London to ship only his books to Longbridge but to bring the rest of his gear to Bath. The clerk said he would see that the message was sent on the next mail coach. Leighton was granted apartments on the second floor overlooking a courtyard garden with a tinkling fountain and lily pool.

He paced the spacious room as the footman set out his shaving gear and hung his coats, setting aside those which would require pressing because of Leighton's hasty packing.

"What is your name?"

"Raymond, sir."

"Perhaps you can help me. I have to find someone, but I know only her maiden name. What advice can you give me?"

"Was she married in Bath?" the fellow asked.

"Yes, I believe so."

"Then perhaps the church registers would have something."

"Churches, there must be dozens of them. I'd run myself silly."

Raymond bowed and nodded at the same time with an almost military click of his heels. "It might take a day, unless luck is with you."

"Would you be willing to look?"

"Certainly."

"Patience Westlake," Leighton said, handing the man a guinea. "She married a merchant about five years ago. But I cannot remember his name."

"Very good, sir," Raymond said with a knowing look as he pocketed the coin and turned to go.

It occurred to Leighton that he ought to correct the man's impression that he was here for a tryst, but he was really too tired to bother. As soon as the room was empty, he threw himself down on the bed and let his tired muscles unclench.

When he had left Longbridge Keep, he'd ridden straight to Ross and Amy's house to make arrangements for taking care of his dependents and to ask if his sister could remember where Patience resided in Bath. She could not help him, so he cautioned them both to say nothing of where he was going. Sadly, he had forgotten to ask her Patience's married name. Perhaps she would not recall it either.

He had no way of writing to Maddie in care of her sisters. He did not have their directions or even their last names. Perhaps he should not have ignored his mother so often when she was reading him the notices in the paper over the breakfast table.

He'd ridden straight through Hereford, then pushed on to Gloucester before stopping for the night. He'd meant to get to Bath yesterday but had put up at Chipping-Sodbury when he realized he was falling asleep on his horse's back. Besides, it was better to arrive here in the day time. The footman would spend his lunch hour locating Patience, and Leighton could call this afternoon.

****

A coughing fit woke him a few hours later, and he knew he must walk to clear his lungs again. He finished the potent contents of Cook's flask and changed his cravat. The scratches on his face were now visible only as two slight red scars, which lent him an air of mystery. Catch him again telling anyone a cat did it. He would claim it was an angry woman.

He was beginning to feel better already. As he ran down the stairs, a momentary dizziness brought him up short. He grabbed the banister and passed a hand across his forehead, but no fever remained. Probably just fatigue. He wandered into the dining room but was told they were done serving luncheon. All he wanted was a brandy and water. The waiter suggested either the card room or the outside tables in the courtyard.

"Excellent." Leighton followed the waiter and seated himself in the sun within sight of the fountain. He let his hat shade his head while the sun baked his back. Pulling out his pocket notebook and a pencil, he jotted down what little he knew of Maddie's relatives. If he had no luck here, he would try York. His mother would expect him to go back to London but would have no idea where to look for him there. Plenty of time to find Maddie.

It suddenly occurred to him that he would have to explain to Maddie that his mother was not in favor of the match either, though she had given no explanation why. The support of his sisters he was sure of, but his mother would not like being displaced by the vicar's daughter and would most certainly show it.

It did not matter. He would take the plunge and smooth things over later. Planning was a good idea, but not over-planning. He should contrive to get a marriage license and keep it handy, in case there might be a time constraint when he did locate Maddie. He had given up by now any thoughts of a normal wedding. Too much confusion anyway, he thought, as he sipped the brandy and water.

Now that the emergency of the bridge was over, he thought of nothing but Maddie. She had the most intriguing pout. You never knew if she was going to laugh or cry. Perhaps she never knew herself. And yet she had a solidity, a durability that he admired. He would never be walking on eggs to talk to her. And his life would be one delightful surprise after another—well, one surprise after another. Perhaps they would not all be delightful—certainly the dead cat had been a stopper. Yet it would always be exciting. He began to hum and before he knew it was jotting scales and notes on the lined paper. He would have to get some proper printed music paper if this melody was going to haunt him. Access to a pianoforte would be helpful but not essential to composition.

After he finished his brandy, he left the hotel and wandered toward the Pump Room, reveling in his freedom. He had never enjoyed London or Lisbon so well. There had been the war to deal with. Now he felt contentment rising in him like a satisfying tide. He had been a great help to Scoville and Wellington. They had said so. He had made a good job of the bridge and nothing terrible had happened to the tenants or livestock in Ross's absence. There would be no more dispatches waiting for him in London, no one asking him to sail off to Spain. Still, much as he enjoyed being footloose, he needed a purpose. Was he using the hunt for Maddie to fill the ache of need he felt when he had no important work to do? He shook his head. No, there was quite another aching need he wanted to satisfy and it had nothing to do with work.

Suddenly he realized he had needed the success of the bridge after his rout by Vicar Westlake. That episode had been more demoralizing than he liked to admit. At least his tenants thought well of him. The poor opinion of the vicar he could live with. Now he needed Maddie. She was like a treat put off for so long he had almost forgotten the taste of her kisses. That meeting in the lane had brought it all back.

When he got to the Pump Room, it was crowded and he saw no one there he knew, just a large group of men to one side. After examining the architectural elements of the room as though he were really interested, he went to the fountain and took an incautious sip of the water, then had a coughing fit. Stares of concern focused on him, and he felt ridiculously conspicuous.

Someone pounded him on the back and he turned to discover…Maddie.

"Leighton. Where did you get such an awful cold?"

"The river," he gasped, wondering that their reunion could take such a mundane turn. He was conscious that a group of men was watching them and that Maddie must have deserted them to come to his aid. "Why did you leave without a word?" he asked.

Her concerned look turned to one of accusation. "But I wrote to you numerous times. Did you get none of my letters? I thought you had forgotten all about me."

"Did you think I would not look for you?" Leighton stared at her finery, the empire-waisted, muslin dress, the frivolous parasol and the fetching bonnet.

"It certainly took you long enough."

He swallowed and tried to get some urgency back into the meeting. "Your father cannot stop us from marrying."

At mention of her father Maddie looked deflated.

"I know that, but not why he is so set against it. There is something he has not told me."

"But how—"

Maddie shushed him as a tall woman with pince-nez approached.

"Leighton Stone," she said, almost tapping her foot with anger.

"Patience? You remember me." Leighton felt himself sweating under the woman's scrutiny.

"How could I forget the boy who rode his pony through my line of washing?"

"No, that was Ross," he corrected.

"Well, you were right after him."

"We were chasing a rabbit," Leighton said, thinking that an adequate defense.

"What the devil are you doing here?" Patience demanded. "If you came for Maddie…"

Leighton managed what he thought was a convincing coughing attack while shaking his head. "Fell in the river and caught a cold. Thought I would come to try the waters."

"Oh, so you are here by accident?" Maddie demanded.

"Yes, how amazing." He winked at Maddie. "I had no notion you were paying Patience a visit."

"Cut line, Leighton," Patience said. "I know why you are here."

Maddie sent him a pained look, and he shrugged, feeling more like a foolish schoolboy than ever.

"Then let me and Maddie have a quiet talk and we shall be able to settle things."

"I am not convinced that would be in her best interest," Patience said, glaring at his face.

He raised a hand to the slight scars, nodded, and scowled.

"May I say something?" Maddie asked.

"Not if you are going to disagree with me," Patience remarked.

"I am almost twenty-one. In a few weeks you cannot stop me from marrying Leighton…*if* I wish to. And if you prevent our meeting, then how will I ever know?"

Leighton's head snapped back toward Maddie. "*If* you wish to?" he asked weakly.

"Shut up, Leighton," his true love said quite brutally. "If Leighton never has a chance to give me a disgust of him, I might elope with him out of sheer desperation, just as you did with George. And it would be your fault."

"We did not elope," Patience said with a defensive look.

"Go on," Leighton said, rolling his hand as he remembered now how logical Maddie could be.

"Whereas if you let us meet to test out our newfound attraction, you may be sure Leighton will do something foolish and I will wash my hands of him."

Leighton watched the wheels turn in the older woman's head and a final look of disgust cross her face.

"You are making game of me, the both of you. Now come, Maddie, or *I* will be the one to wash my hands of *you*," Patience said.

"Nothing would be more to my purpose," Leighton replied, reaching for Maddie's arm.

Patience turned again and put her hands on her hips. "Very well. As long as Maddie is staying with me, you may call from one to two in the afternoon—and at no other time."

"See you tomorrow," Maddie said as she followed her sister. She winked at him and Leighton found himself smiling foolishly until a thought hit him.

"Wait. I don't know where you live."

Patience smiled fiendishly as she led her sister away.

Leighton thought of following them at a distance, but a portly gentleman blocked his path.

"That was an interesting way to get an introduction

to the most beautiful girl in Bath," the man said with the slightest of accents. He was of middle age and meaty but powerful.

"Do I know you?" Leighton asked, starting to step around the man but hesitating at the familiar tone.

"Actually, you do. I was attached to the Surgeon-General's staff in Lisbon. Dr. Murray."

"Yes, now I remember." Leighton shook his hand but listened to the doctor with only half his attention as he looked wistfully after the departing women.

"As I recall, I extracted a ball from between your ribs. How is the wound?"

"Fine. Oh, the occasional twinge, but—could you excuse me? I really must—"

"Royal Crescent."

Leighton's eyes snapped back to the man's florid face. "What?"

"She lives at Number 6 Royal Crescent."

"Thank you. I did not mean to be rude, but…"

"Say no more. I believe you are staying at Prad's Hotel. I thought I saw you in the lobby."

"Yes, I am."

"Perhaps we can have dinner together."

"That would be delightful," Leighton said, thinking it would be anything but, if this man started to chat about Peninsular days. "Ah, could I ask that you not mention meeting me in Lisbon? It's a bit of a long story, but the upshot is my family have no idea I ever left the country, so I would be in the suds if they found out."

Murray regarded him appraisingly. "Say no more. In my profession, I know how to be discreet. How about tonight?"

"Tonight?"

"Dinner?"

"Yes, of course. Say eight o'clock?"

"Capital. Come to my room. It's the first one overlooking the courtyard on the second floor."

At first Leighton thought it strange that he should run into the doctor here, but there were, at one time or another, probably a hundred thousand Englishmen engaged in the fighting in Spain. Perhaps it was not so odd to run into one of them in Bath. Certainly it was a lucrative setting for a doctor.

He paused on the street and pulled out his notebook to jot down the address. He saw his scribbling from the afternoon and began to hum the tune over in his head. He wondered how Maddie would like it. Now that his chief worry was over, he could spare some time for things like composition. With Maddie for inspiration, music would be easy to write.

Chapter Seven

Maddie was sitting in the walled garden behind her sister's town house, relieved that Leighton really cared. He had not seemed all that smitten, but he *had* come, and with that wretched cold. If only she could talk to him without Patience glaring at them over her spectacles. She was wondering if it would be possible to slip out and see him, but realized she had no idea where he was staying. Then she heard him, counting out loud as he had used to do when teaching her music. When his voice got to six he stopped and began to fiddle with the catch on the neighbor's back gate.

Maddie stood on the bench by the boxwood hedge and spotted Leighton glancing up at the neighbor's windows. "Leighton," she hissed, "what are you doing?"

"Breaking into your sister's garden."

"Well, you miscounted and if you rouse Mr. Glasden's pug, you will be sorry. Wait there." She ran to the back gate, undid the latch, pushed it open, and shut it behind her before her sister's dog could wake up from its nap. Leighton tossed his hat aside, reached for Maddie, and drew her into an embrace and kiss that stilled her doubts even as it made her heart race.

"God, I missed you," he said, then stepped back to look at her. His hungry gaze caressed her in a way that made her breath catch in her throat. Perhaps it was the new gown and hair ribbons, but he actually made her feel attractive.

"Why did it take you so long to come?" It was not what she had meant to say, but his delay did require some sort of explanation. She searched his face and saw the tiredness in it.

"Well, I had a flood on my hands. The bridge washed away and I had to build a new one." He shook his head and ran one hand through his deep chestnut hair. "Damn it, Maddie, I've had a rough two weeks of it."

She looked up at him with concern. "A flood? But if the bridge is gone, no one can get to old Mrs. Peterson's house."

"I sent a boy to check on her, and she is fine."

"But Leighton, if you are here, who is taking care of all your dependents?"

"Amy and Ross. I should have saddled them with the responsibility from the beginning, not you."

"But I was glad to do it, to be of some use. No one thought it odd of me."

"They all thought you were doing it because I planned for you to be mistress of Longbridge someday."

"So you always meant to marry me?" She stepped back from him in confusion. He had never given her any hint of this.

"That was my plan if things worked out."

Leighton reached for her again, but she stepped away from him.

"I think you might have mentioned it to me. For someone who spent all his time clerking, you are not at all good at communication. You never answered a single letter since I've been here."

Leighton sighed. "Did I not just tell you the bridge was out? Nat brought a sack of mail back from the village while I was packing, but Susan said there was nothing from you. I especially asked her."

Maddie blew out an impatient breath. It had been as she'd feared. "But who actually sorted through it? Susan?"

Leighton looked stricken. "I don't know, only that Susan came to say there was nothing for me except bills."

Maddie turned away. "Nothing your mother wanted you to open, at any rate."

Leighton smacked his palm to his forehead. "Oh, God. I would have known you were safe instead of just guessing where you were." He swept her into his arms again. "When I get home…"

"Forget your mother. I do not care what she did, now that you are here. But I have had to take so much on faith."

"I offered to marry you." He kissed the top of her head. "Surely you knew I would come for you."

She glanced down at her new cream dress. "I hoped you would come."

She saw he was ready to protest his faithfulness, so she pressed her fingers to his lips and said slowly, so that even a dolt could understand, "Just tell me this. Do you really love me?"

He cupped her fingers in his rough hand and kissed them, pulling a sigh from her. "Yes, and I want you for my wife."

"Then I will let nothing stop us, even if it means a runaway match, even if Patience hates me forever."

Leighton hugged her again and sighed, feeling the soft ringlets of her hair entangling his fingers, just as her smile had ensnared his heart. "Why don't they want us together? Have you any clue?"

She froze in his arms. "No, and it does seem very odd. When I mentioned you to Patience, I was sure she knew more than she was telling, but you cannot get anything out of her when she is on her guard."

"Well, at least she is going to let me call. Will she stand up with us? I can get a license tomorrow."

"Without Papa's permission, we still have to wait until I am of age."

He caressed her cheek with his knuckles. "That is only two weeks. We have been waiting for each other for years without knowing it."

"Yes, what is two weeks in the grand scheme of things?" Maddie looked up at him. "How long have you known?"

"That I loved you?" Leighton held her face in his hands. "I think since I was a boy."

"But you never said anything, not even in your letters. So you could not really have known until that day in the lane."

"The war…was in the way. I always meant to marry you. I was just afraid something would happen to prevent it." He thought about telling her about Spain but knew it was the wrong moment.

"Such as your mother," she said.

"I shall take care of Mother. You are not to mind anything she says that might be rude or cutting, for she treats everyone the same."

"I know."

She toyed with his lapels, giving Leighton a strange sense of her ownership of him. He had all this time been thinking of Maddie as his wife, as the dependent one, when actually he suspected she would be the one in charge of their marriage. Yes, he was sure of it. And no, he did not mind a bit.

"I just wonder what would have happened if we had not met that day," she said softly.

"The very same." He smoothed back a ringlet of hair that had escaped her ribbon. "I was on my way to see you."

"So that was your intention, to ask me to marry you?" She scanned his face.

"Yes. Why are you so worried?"

"I thought it might have been some sort of…gallant whim."

He chuckled. "No, before I had any idea what marriage was all about, I pictured us together."

"I did as well." Maddie drew closer, and he kissed her tentatively at first, then with more ardor, his hands encircling her waist as she twined her arms around his neck.

Maddie gasped when she heard Patience calling her. "I must go. See you tomorrow at one."

"I shall be here." Leighton remembered to duck when Patience came out to find Maddie.

He was glad he had come to see her now rather than wait for tomorrow. He had always thought he was the one who was not sure of himself, but she had been grieving because he had not come for her sooner. He should have let the bridge go and put Maddie first. He would not make the same mistake again.

He went back to the hotel and left word at the desk to send someone to awaken him at seven. Then he went upstairs and stretched out on the bed.

As it turned out, the footman who came to awaken him was Raymond.

"Mrs. Patience Carter lives at 6 Royal Crescent."

"Thank you, Raymond. Excellent." He gave the man a guinea. It would never have occurred to Leighton to tell the man he had found the information out by other means.

"She's a widow, but I saw her. If you don't mind my saying so, sir—not your type."

"No, but her sister is."

"Ah." Raymond gave a nod of understanding and helped Leighton back into his coat before he left. Leighton went to Dr. Murray's rooms as arranged, content to renew his acquaintance with the man now that he was sure he had an understanding with Maddie.

"I hope you do not mind that I already ordered our meal," Murray said as he supervised the laying of the first course on a round table in the middle of the sitting room.

"Not at all. I have been so caught up in my quest, I have not given much thought to food lately."

They seated themselves, and the doctor carved the duck for them.

"Quite a change from the fare in Portugal or Spain," Murray said as he served him a slice of fowl, crisp and juicy.

"I remember eating while I was there, but I have no clear idea now what it was."

"You youngsters, more appetite for fighting than food."

Leighton stared at him, trying to assess his purpose. Was it just to talk over old times, or something more? "Not in my case." Leighton sensed the doctor wanted more conversation from him, for the elaborate dinner, the favor of the address. Still, the man was not ready yet to tell him what.

The doctor raised an eyebrow, but before he could speak, Leighton said, "I cannot place your accent. I keep thinking Prussian, but it's not that."

"I am Flemish."

"Ah, that explains it." Leighton took a bite of duck. "Excellent."

"I joined the English at Wagram, but I am retired now. You, on the other hand, were never in the regular army."

"No, I was not," Leighton said, breaking a piece of bread. He could be just as evasive.

"That did not keep the French sniper from getting you, did it?"

"Why he chose me, I have no idea."

"They knew there was something special about a man not in uniform. Not a common soldier, possibly an officer. He knew you were someone important."

Leighton put on his most charming smile. "But I was not important. Just had a curiosity to visit the front."

Murray had drunk two glasses of wine already and swung his head toward Leighton, casting him a dubious look. "Five years running?"

And he thought he'd kept a low profile. Leighton swallowed and licked his lips. "I have a lot of curiosity."

"I saw you with Scoville. You are the one they call the *music master*. Yes, you played for their balls and entertainments, but you went there to help Scoville with the codes."

Leighton felt a creeping shiver but waited until he had finished. There was only one way to handle such sure knowledge of his vocation. "Oh, that," he said lightly. "It was an amusing pastime. I am not sure how much help I was."

"Hah, you are a cool one. Any other man would have parlayed that work into a diplomatic appointment. Instead you disappear."

"But I have not disappeared, merely resumed my normal life, part of which will be to marry."

"The young lady in question. Constance Westlake." Murray raised his glass in a toast.

Leighton tapped his glass to the other lightly. "Maddie, my childhood friend."

Murray resumed his meal, chewing like a ruminating cow. "Does she know what you did during the war?"

"No, I told you, nor does my family. Of course, I would prefer to keep it that way."

"There should be no big secret about it now. Why so modest?"

"I am not exactly sure." Leighton took another bite and chewed even more slowly than the doctor. "Perhaps I have come to enjoy their disapproval of me. It is a way of being bad that requires no real effort."

The doctor laughed. "You are an odd one. I knew it when I dug that ball out of your side. You just looked at me as though to say, 'Get on with it.' I says to myself, 'Here is a lad who is used to pain, used to the thought of death waiting around the corner for him. Now how comes this to be?' I have always been a curious man, myself."

"So that is why you invited me here," Leighton blurted out, making the doctor laugh again.

"Yes, my advocation is to study people, to find out what makes them work. I always do figure them out, but you have remained a question mark all these years."

"Perhaps I can satisfy your curiosity." Leighton refilled their wine glasses. "What do you want to know?"

"I have seen men hardened by war. You were not one of those. You were shot the day you arrived."

"The day before. We encountered a French frigate, and a sniper in the rigging got me. But we were so far away the ball was mostly spent when it hit me."

"So you carried that in your side for a day. But you knew your life was in no danger from it?"

"On the contrary, I had the gravest concerns about encountering an incompetent surgeon."

Murray raised an eyebrow and was about to reply when the waiters arrived with the second course. Leighton feigned an interest in the dishes this time, engaging the serving men in some discussion of the standing rack of lamb. He could see Murray's impatience building.

"What were we talking about?" Leighton asked as the doctor sliced off a portion of the chops and placed them on his plate.

Murray raised an eyebrow, still holding the carving knife. "You were speaking about your fear of an incompetent surgeon."

"Oh, yes." Leighton took a bite and chewed it well before swallowing and pointing his knife at the doctor. "Instead, I met you."

The man chuckled. "You are lucky I agreed to lower myself to the duties of surgeon. Or would you have just cut the ball out yourself?"

"Or left it," Leighton said as he cut another bite and chewed methodically.

"So you had met death before the war. Where?"

Leighton laid his silverware down and picked up his

wine glass. "In my childhood bed. I have a reputation in my family, an undeserved one, for weak lungs. It's simply that if I am in a room full of smoke my lungs will rebel and fill up with fluid."

"Let me guess. There was always smoke in the rooms at your home."

"Yes. I remember one night in particular when I woke up gasping for air. I got up and leaned over to open the window and I felt my lungs fall forward and slap against the inside of my chest. You can imagine how that made my heart race. I crept down to the kitchen. Cook took one look at me, wrapped me in a blanket, and mixed up some concoction that saved me."

"How old were you then?"

"Eleven. Now you tell me, how close was I to death?"

"Very close." The doctor sat back with a sigh and emptied his glass. "What happened to you this time?"

"I was building a bridge and inhaled some river water."

Murray nodded, accepting Leighton's explanation at face value.

"But recuperating is not why I am in Bath."

"No, your pursuit of Miss Westlake. Has she any idea what kind of man you are?"

"We knew each other as children. Anything that has happened in the intervening years cannot matter so much." Leighton pushed his plate aside with satisfaction. So that was all the doctor wanted, to solve a puzzle. He had never considered himself a mystery before.

"Oh, I did not mean about your exploits." Murray carefully refilled both their glasses. "I meant about your provoking pauses."

Leighton smiled. "Maddie and I used to play music together." He took a sip of the wine and smiled at the doctor. "She already knows the rests are as important as the notes."

Chapter Eight

The next morning, Leighton visited his horses. He judged that Chandros needed a run, so he took the younger horse on a gallop into the country, up the old Roman road, then worked his way around the north end of the city, finally meeting the stage road that had brought him there. Chandros gave a satisfied grunt as though he recognized it too. Leighton was always amazed at a horse's sense of direction. If a beast had a home, it could always find its way back. If, like Chandros, all it had was a stall somewhere, it still tried to find it again. He patted the colt's neck.

"Soon you will have fields of your own, with mares to cover, and will think no more of roaming the countryside."

When he returned to his room, it was past eleven, and he discovered that his man Tibbs had taken possession of his suite.

"S'pose you chose this place for the horses' convenience," the wiry valet growled as he looked up from pressing one of Leighton's shirts.

"Yes, of course," Leighton said, realizing it might irritate his man. He tossed his hat and gloves on the small table in the entryway, a table Tibbs had just cleaned of maps and papers. The grizzled man stared at him, pursing his lips but saying nothing.

"It has a lovely garden where you can have lunch."

"How delightful," Tibbs said, his broad London accent sounding oddly shaped around those words. "I've brought you your mail. There's a bit of it."

Leighton groaned and sat at the small desk near the sitting room window, slitting open the various letters and packets that were piled there. He decided his remove from London to Bath, rather than Longbridge Keep, might ensure Tibbs would stay in his employ for a time. The man had been less than enthusiastic about a permanent move to the country.

Why Leighton wanted to hang onto the acerbic retainer was a puzzle to him, except that Tibbs did not smother him as his mother attempted to do. He was far more likely to give him the sharp side of his tongue as Maddie did. Leighton paused, gave a heavy sigh, and conjured up Maddie's face, those pouting lips and expectant green eyes. He would see her again in a few short hours.

A coughing fit overtook him, as it sometimes did after he had been doing something strenuous. A small glass of brandy appeared in front of him, and he took it gratefully from Tibbs's weathered hand. The pungent liquid seemed to ease the cough, and he thanked the man.

"Wise choice, Bath. Perhaps you can shake that nasty cold ye've taken."

Leighton cast Tibbs a suspicious look. Could it be that the man actually cared about him? He shook his head. Tibbs was probably just being sarcastic.

"I did not come here to take the waters."

"Oh, really?"

"I came for Maddie Westlake, my fiancée." Leighton was carefully setting aside notes from London friends he must answer, while tossing to the floor invitations to London events, either past or future, to which he need not reply.

"This is the parson's daughter?" Tibbs asked, carefully folding a freshly ironed shirt. "I thought she lived at Longbridge."

"She does—did. She is visiting her sister. As soon as we are married, I plan to remove to Longbridge and stay there." Leighton sent him a challenging look.

"Never to go to London again?" Tibbs asked with a scowl at the pile of discarded mail on the floor.

"Actually, we have to take a house there next year, for the whole season, for Susan's come out. I was hoping you would manage that for me."

"The whole lot of them down on us, with company to boot?"

"Afraid so," Leighton mused as he discarded another invitation.

"We shall see," Tibbs promised.

Leighton knew better than to press him for a definite answer. He'd had no breakfast and had not been invited by Patience to luncheon, so he must make haste if he wanted anything to eat before he called on Maddie. He cast off his riding coat and pulled a blue swallowtail out of the armoire. Tibbs watched him resentfully as Leighton stripped off his neckcloth and shirt and replaced them with fresh garments. Leighton was almost dressed again when he realized he had put on the ones the man had just ironed and folded but he refrained from laughter. He did not want to bring on another coughing fit. Tibbs dutifully helped him into the coat.

"I may be back before dinner."

"And I may be here."

Leighton suppressed his chuckle until he was

descending the stairs.

He wandered into the garden, where only a lady and a man were sitting having a late breakfast. So he seated himself, and Raymond appeared as if by magic. Leighton ordered ham, eggs, bread, and tea. He wanted to be sober for this interview.

He had chosen a small table under a dogwood just done blooming, and he swept a few dried blossoms off the opposing chair so he could lay his hat down. The fountain was not one of those disgusting mineral springs but a cool trickle of water that came from the mouth of a gargoyle-like green man's face. It puddled in a basin of water lilies with fish swimming under the shade of the leaves.

Raymond brought the tea and Leighton poured a cup, closing his eyes to listen to the rhythm of the water, thinking it must have a pattern since it ran over the same surfaces again and again. The pattering and bubbles were not totally random. At most, the spring had three or four notes in its repertoire, but it was enough. He drew a blank sheet of paper out of his card case and began to play with the notes, trying them out in his mind, hoping for some coherent melody.

Now that he had found Maddie, he could not think of anything else. She had doubted him, he was sure of it. And why not? He had delayed so long she was justified in giving up on him. He had always taken his love for her for granted, and he had been arrogant enough to assume she'd felt the same. That had been a mistake. He must never let her doubt him again. In some ways, Maddie was unsure of herself, probably because of her father. Obviously she had no idea how lovely and precious she was.

The melody came to him. It matched the notes from the fountain, clear and pure as Maddie's voice. He jotted down the beginning lines of music as he watched the carp going about their business under the surface of the pool. The water splashed down the stones into the pond and gave them a perpetual sheen of coolness. He saw Maddie running barefoot though the meadow and tried to remember the occasion. But there were so many days he had not treasured as he should have. He remembered Maddie holding his sister's first child and looking hopeful, her face flushing the palest of pinks like the roses in the garden. He remembered her picking violets with dew on her lashes, but that had been when they were young and he had not understood his feelings for her. Now he knew every look of her face. He had stored those visions in his mind to hold him through the cold hard times in Spain.

The waiter brought his food, and he laid aside the page of notes. She had waited, perhaps not by choice or chance. Her father had meant to keep her chained to the vicarage the rest of her days. Leighton had abetted him in that by expecting her to do his work of supporting the poor and aged. But Maddie had a mind of her own. If he slighted her again, she might very well refuse him.

He must woo her, convince her she was the single most important thing in his life. The music would take some time, so he vowed to get her a present. A ring was something she would have to choose, but a set of pearls, perhaps. He had no experience of entrancing young ladies, had always avoided them, in fact. Suddenly he dropped his fork and took up the pen again as the music floated through his mind with the clarity of real sound. His pencil moved along the paper like feet treading a well-worn path.

Maddie would not be won by any material gifts, but his music—that might do it. He took the last sip of his tea, and the waiter appeared magically from nowhere to pour him another cup. So he was not really alone but was being watched. He wondered if the man thought he was a composer who came to Bath only to work on his latest pieces. Leighton laughed. The yews shrugged heavenward with branches like praying hands, and Leighton enjoyed the illusion that everything was in accord with him, that his future was assured.

****

Maddie went to look out the window of the morning room for the tenth time since luncheon.

"A watched pot never boils," her sister said from her seat at the escritoire.

"What has that got to do with Leighton being late?"

"Nothing, but you shouldn't seem so eager to him."

"So you are not opposed to an alliance with him?"

Patience bit her lip thoughtfully. "Yes, I am. There is much in the past that speaks against it. Nothing but grief will come of it, but…"

"But you don't see how you can stop me," Maddie concluded, getting down from her kneeling position on the window seat and checking her skirt for wrinkles.

"You were ever the impetuous one."

Maddie crossed the room and seated herself primly on the sofa. "I see no reason against the marriage."

"How will it make Papa feel?"

"It should make him feel secure."

"But he doesn't even like working in Leighton's keep, not after—"

"Not after what?" Maddie demanded. There was

80

that unknown disagreement rearing its head again. "Why won't you tell me?"

"Not after he had words with Leighton's father."

"Leighton is not his father, though he is like him. Perhaps Papa has too much pride to work for any man without resenting it."

Patience arched an eyebrow. "He would be offended to hear you accuse him of the sin of pride."

"He is always in a state of offense. I do not think the world was meant to be such a grim place. At least I did not think so until Mother and Lord Longbridge died."

Patience got a look on her face, as though on the point of saying more.

Her butler tapped on the door, then announced Leighton.

"Sorry I am so late." He smiled as he entered and crossed to Maddie. "I had some shopping to do."

"Shopping?" Maddie complained.

"For you," he said, presenting her with a long jeweler's box.

Patience rose. "Leighton, it is not at all—"

She stopped dead when Leighton also handed her a box, then glared at him as she opened it.

"Look, Patience, pearls," Maddie said. "Aren't they the loveliest? Oh, you have a set too! Help me try them on, Leighton."

As he moved to place the strand around his beloved's neck, Patience brushed him aside.

"I shall do that."

"I know you will *both* look lovely in them."

Maddie realized that he was trying to get in Patience's good graces to make sure she would be allowed to keep such a gift.

Leighton faltered, seeming to search about in his mind. "I missed so many of your birthdays and other occasions. I was just trying to make up for my neglect of you—*both* of you."

"This more than serves the purpose." Patience did not don her pearls but looked at them in their box with a certain softening of her face.

"And...and I wanted to invite you to tea at my hotel."

"That is out of the question," the older sister said. "I told you that you could see Maddie here in my townhouse, but calling on you at your hotel is entirely inappropriate."

"But we would not be alone. Dr. Murray will be there. And it is not in the hotel but in the charming garden outside. There is a pond there like the one you used to have in your back yard at the vicarage."

"Please, Patience," Maddie begged. "Leighton and I have hardly gotten to talk at all."

"Very well, we shall take tea with you on our way to the Pump Room today."

"You will like the garden. I started—"

The butler opened the door to announce Mrs. Scrope-Nevins, and Leighton wondered if Patience had invited the woman to foil his plans. But since the thin lady seemed totally caught up in conversation with Maddie's sister, she served rather to distract her from her chaperonage.

"I thought you would never come," Maddie whispered as he took a seat on the sofa beside her.

"I would have bought you a ring, but you need to try that sort of thing on for yourself. When can we go pick one out?"

"We usually shop in the morning, on Fleet Street. But first we go to the lending library. Wait for us there at ten o'clock."

"I can pretend I encountered you by accident and take you past the jeweler's."

Maddie felt the pearls. "They must have been very dear, Leighton. And you had to buy two sets."

"It is about time I got to enjoy some of my fortune. You look beautiful."

"It must be the dress." Maddie smoothed the peach muslin.

"Oh, no, you would look lovely in nothing."

Maddie stared at Leighton until he realized what he'd said, then gave a gurgle of laughter.

"I meant *anything*," he corrected.

Patience looked up. "Has Leighton made a fool of himself yet?"

"Yes, Patience."

Chapter Nine

Leighton had seen the tea table laid, then gone to the hotel lobby to wait for Maddie and Patience. He hoped Dr. Murray would heed the obvious panic in his note begging him to join them. If not, he could always use the doctor's patients as an excuse. When Maddie and Patience came into the hotel, the older sister looked suspiciously around the lobby while Leighton's favorite footman conducted them toward the garden as though it was the most normal arrangement in the world. Leighton came behind them and gave him a wink, then slipped him another coin.

"It is lovely," Maddie said when he'd led her to the pond. She gazed at the water lilies, then whisked her fingers through the water. "May we feed the fish?"

"Fish?" Patience asked.

Leighton took her elbow to help her over the rough stone of the courtyard. "Yes. Do you see them under the water-lily leaves? They hide out there in the heat of the day."

Patience nodded and smiled. For the first time, Leighton thought he could see a resemblance between her and her beautiful mother.

"They do remind me of home."

"Whatever happened to your ornamental pond?" Leighton asked.

Maddie looked up at him, a crease between her

delicate brows. "Papa had it filled in after Mother died. He erected that awful sundial."

"Hmm, I wonder why."

"Because your father gave her the fish," Maddie said. "Papa never liked them."

Patience turned her back on the pond and went to the table with its white cloth and plates of tea cakes. The smile was gone from her face and Leighton began to question the wisdom of reminding her of the vicarage. He pulled out a chair for Patience and stood watching Maddie run her hands in the water of the fountain.

He remembered his father bringing back from Hereford fish in a pail for the vicarage pond. Why had the vicar so resented this kindness?

Maddie came to join them, glancing down at her dress, Leighton guessed to make sure she had not snagged it.

"Don't worry, though," she said as she sat down.

"About what?" He still had his hands on the back of her chair and she canted her head sideways to look up at him, her glossy brown locks curling over her shoulder.

"The fish. I caught them all and moved them to your dam. Probably they do better there."

Leighton nodded and sat down, realizing this must have been a Herculean task since his dam sat no less than two miles from the vicarage. No doubt she had been forced to sneak about to save the fish, too. He tried to think of any other reasons the vicar should hate him and his family.

The waiter brought the tea tray then, and for a few moments they were engaged in getting their tea. Besides the tea, bread, and cakes, there was a decanter of sherry and one of brandy.

Maddie took a bite of buttered bread and sighed. "Everything tastes so much better out of doors. Why is that?"

"I do not know, but you are right," he agreed.

"The air smells much better," Patience said. "Not stale indoor air but warm air mingled with the scent of the pines and the herbs and flowers."

Maddie looked toward the fountain. "It's the sound of the water, too, and the birds. Leighton, listen…always the same pattern of sounds. Do they repeat?"

"Yes, I was listening to it at lunchtime."

"Could a fountain play its own music?" Maddie asked.

Leighton smiled. They thought so much alike. "If you designed it right. Perhaps I'll redirect a channel from the stream and put a fountain in the old courtyard at home."

Maddie wrinkled her nose. "Your mother won't like that."

"Mother doesn't like anything."

Patience glanced at Leighton over her pince-nez. "She won't like you two seeing each other. That's for certain. She wants Leighton to marry a fashionable lady, not a parson's daughter."

"But your mother was a Gaines. I cannot see why she would object so strongly."

Patience glanced away, and Leighton caught sight of his new friend looking rather heated. "Murray. You were able to join us after all."

"Sorry I am late. I was waylaid by Sally Pierce."

"That gossip-monger," Patience said. "No need to introduce the doctor, Leighton. We are well acquainted."

"Then may I present Patience's sister, Maddie?"

86

"Two charming names in one sentence," the doctor said with a bow.

"Let me help you to tea and bread…or some brandy, if you'd rather," Patience said to the doctor, as she took charge of the meal.

"Is it all right if I show Maddie the rest of the garden?" Leighton asked.

Patience looked over her shoulder. "How far does it go?"

"Just over to that wall."

"Oh, very well."

Leighton led Maddie on a tour of the herb beds and whispered. "I think she is softening toward me."

"You showing me a garden is not a good ruse. Do you know anything about plants?"

"No, but she must know that—still she let us go anyway."

"You always could charm her."

"But not you. You see through me."

"Before you went away, I thought I knew you." Maddie turned and looked up at him. "But Leighton, is this all for real? Are we really to be married?"

He stared at her, then pulled her hand more securely though his arm. "Absolutely. What gives you such doubts?"

"When I wake up in the morning, I have to convince myself all over again that it really is going to happen."

"What can possibly stand in our way?"

Maddie glanced around the walled garden but did not seem to derive from her surroundings the same sort of serenity they instilled in Leighton.

"I don't know. But I have the most awful feeling that something will prevent it."

"Well, I do not think it will be your sister. In fact, she seems half taken with Dr. Murray. If we had more separating us from them than a single yew tree, I would pull you into my arms and kiss you."

"But why, Leighton?"

"Because that is what engaged couples do."

"No, be serious. Why marry me when you know what it will do to our parents?"

Leighton pulled her down onto a bench, still within Patience's hawk-like gaze but small enough that Maddie had to sit thigh to thigh with him. "Because I love you. No matter where I was, I thought only of you."

"But you were only in London." Maddie had that slight scowl on her brow that made her look both innocent and serious at the same time.

"Oh, well…" Leighton realized there was no need to keep anything from her anymore. "That is not exactly true. I did have to make some trips. I thought I should mention it, in case Dr. Murray lets slip about seeing me."

"Seeing you where?"

"Lisbon or…Madrid?" He said it as a question but that did not stop the storm of resentment he saw brewing on Maddie's delicate brow.

"Lisbon, Portugal?" she asked in a fierce whisper.

"Why, yes." He could feel his heart thudding in his chest as she digested this information.

"And just how much time did you spend in the Peninsula?"

Leighton tried to capture her hand, but she snatched it away.

"Not much above four or five…months," he said limply. "Perhaps a year."

"So all those letters you wrote were lies? How you

were too busy to come home? How you had to stay in London?"

Her anger he could have taken, but this tearful accusation cut him to the heart. "Well, not at the drop of a hat. Winters were always slow for campaigning. I was home almost every winter."

"You were not even on the same continent most of the time," she accused. "And that is why it took so long for you to reply."

Her flushed cheeks and luminous eyes spoke of a heart about to crack, and he could not even take her in his arms to comfort her. "You sound angry."

"I *am* angry," she said as she wadded her handkerchief in her lap.

Leighton watched her eyes hunt among the plants and wondered why she was so upset now that it was all over. She should have been glad to have been protected from this worry.

"And did you stay in the cities? Tell me the truth." The glare from her green eyes pierced him.

"Most of the time. I had to make some trips into the interior."

"Where the fighting was."

He swiped a hand across his brow. "I had no control over that."

"For God's sake, Leighton. Why didn't you tell me?"

"I am telling you."

"Why didn't you tell me while it was happening? I thought you didn't even care about me, that I was just a bother to you."

"I did not want to worry you."

"You idiot! I worried about you anyway. At least

then my fears would have had a direction, instead of just being a vague unease."

"I am sorry. But if you were worried, that means that you loved me too." Once again he tried to capture her hands, but she withdrew them and stood up.

"Of course I loved you. Now, I'm not so sure. No woman wants a husband she cannot trust."

"But I was sworn to secrecy," Leighton protested. "If I had written to you and my letter had been—"

"When have I ever betrayed your confidence?" She folded her arms in front of her, a sure sign he was in trouble.

"Never, and if only you knew how much I needed your help with the codes." He stood and spoke quietly, hoping to keep their altercation secret from Patience.

"Codes? What sort of work was this?" She was intently scanning his face.

"I was helping Scoville. He was Wellington's code-breaker."

Maddie looked into his eyes and apparently found no more lies there.

"Do your mother and sisters know?"

Leighton knew it was the wrong thing to say, but if she caught him in any sort of lie she might never forgive him. "No, only my brother-in-law."

"You told Ross and not me?" Her lips trembled at this new betrayal and she turned away.

She paced to the pond, staring down at the fish, telling herself that at least he was confessing now, before they went any closer toward marriage. But was that what he thought she wanted, to be shielded? Leighton should know her better than that.

She heard his boots scrape on the stones of the

courtyard. "Maddie?"

"It figures you would tell another man and not me."

"I had to tell someone in case…in case anything happened."

She spun toward him. "Oh, so we would know where your body was buried."

"Listen to me, Maddie. It was not your discretion I feared but the post. If any of my letters had been intercepted…"

"You could have written me in code."

She thought he looked surprised but then he smiled. "I wish I had thought of that."

"But you did not, like so many other things." She turned and walked toward the table, noting a slight smile on her sister's face. But whether it was because of her fight with Leighton, or some tidbit the doctor had whispered in Patience's ear, she could not be sure. She was surprised that her sister was drinking sherry but not at all shocked that the doctor had broached the brandy.

"Are you ready to go to the Pump Room, sister?"

"Yes," Maddie replied. She was in so much inner turmoil she needed some time alone. But one often could find solitude for reflection in the midst of a crowd of people when one could not with just one companion.

"Dr. Murray will walk us down. No need for Leighton to trouble himself."

As they left through the lobby, Maddie glanced back once. When she saw how miserable Leighton looked, she almost went back to him. She would forgive him, of course, but they must have an understanding. He could not be hiding things from her. She was not like his mother or his younger sister, always having to be protected. She thought about sending him a note saying as much, but she was sure he meant to call again tomorrow even if they did not meet the next morning on Fleet Street. She would have to find a way for them to have a moment alone.

After that, her moments of reflection in the Pump Room were severely hampered by the arrival of old Mrs. Marsden, her daughter Lady Haddon, and her granddaughter Dierdra. The grandmother was a patient of Dr. Murray's, so they fell into instant consultation. Patience renewed her acquaintance with Lady Hadden, and Maddie was obliged to amuse Dierdra. After half an hour, Maddie had a throb in her head that had nothing to do with Leighton, but she had realized one thing. She had always thought of Leighton as perfect, or nearly so. That he had some of the same flaws as other men should have been no surprise to her. But he would have to acknowledge that what he had done was wrong, not argue with her about it.

Chapter Ten

Leighton rode Chandros again in the morning, farther into the hills this time, taking some of the side roads and cart tracks. Familiarizing himself with the geography of a place was a habit he had picked up in Spain. You could never tell when knowing where a road led might save your life.

He then spent an hour touring several of the jewelers' establishments. Of course, there was the family heirloom ring, an amethyst set in gold, but he did not want to try to pry that off his mother's finger. He was sure Maddie would prefer to choose her own jewelry…if she would still marry him at all, or even speak to him after yesterday's debacle.

Yet he could not think that finally confessing his part in the war had been a mistake. He had actually hoped Maddie would admire him for what he had accomplished. Far from it, she had very nearly ditched him then and there. So why had he tried to defend himself? Clearly he should have owned to his fault and begged her forgiveness. At least that hurdle was past them. And he was glad he had not let the deception run on any longer. Better to confess than have her find out from someone else. Whether anyone else found out now was immaterial. If was only Maddie's opinion that counted.

He did not run up against them while shopping,

though he had looked for them. Either Maddie was very angry with him or their plans had changed. He had a sensation of being watched that went beyond the residents scrutinizing him with their quizzing glasses as a newcomer. By now, Patience would have had time to write to her father. Leighton was going to have to decide what he would do if Vicar Westlake confronted him on a Bath Street and demanded he leave town. He would not leave, of course, but such an altercation would not be good for Maddie's reputation. Patience's actions did not jump with her tattling to her father, but old habits died hard. She had taken Maddie in on command. What if Westlake had also told her to let him know if Leighton showed up?

When he returned to his rooms, his valet was polishing his evening shoes and handed him a thick packet of papers. It was addressed simply to Mr. Stone, Prad's Hotel.

"I didn't think anyone knew I was here." Leighton opened the bundle on the small table near the door. There was something oddly familiar about the bold lettering on the outside sheet but his name was not written in cursive, so he could not recognize the hand. He extracted a sheaf of sheet music—some was printed in America, some was in French—and as he leafed through, he found one very badly handwritten page of music.

"Did this come in the post?"

"No, not the post."

Leighton waited in vain for clarification. "From where then?"

"A servant delivered it."

"Whose servant?"

Tibbs thought for a moment. "I have no idea."

Leighton groaned. "There is no return address. Didn't this servant say anything?"

"Had an odd accent. If I was to hazard a guess, I'd say he was…American."

Leighton knew there was no point in trying to get any more out of Tibbs. The man was still punishing him for dragging him out of London. He turned the packet over and over, looking for some clue to its origin. Perhaps a military acquaintance had been posted to America and had sent him these scores. Certainly the war with America was still in full force. But there was no enclosure letter, which seemed damned odd. And how would such a person know he was at this hotel…or in Bath at all? Leighton cast the printed pages aside, then scrutinized the handwritten piece.

"Tibbs, where's my cello?"

He heard a scrape and looked up to see Tibbs wrestling the cello case through the doorway.

"You brought it. Good." Leighton threw the case open on the floor.

"You did say send only the books to your estate."

Leighton ignored Tibbs' rare example of explicit obedience, removed the instrument and tuned it, then tried to master the notes on the page. He saw Tibbs flinch and got a chill himself from the scraping. This could not really be music. So what was it?

Leighton laid the cello to rest again. He folded the handwritten piece and put it in his notebook, thinking he might recognize the handwriting when he had more time.

He had something of a coughing attack on his way down to the courtyard garden as he recalled he had left poor Tibbs to put the instrument away again. He definitely had to treat the man with more consideration if he wanted to keep him.

He asked the waiter for a brandy and water with his luncheon, got the same table where they had tea yesterday, and gave a sigh of relief when the brandy arrived. He couldn't help wondering if there were any traps in the way of his engagement other than his mother, Maddie's father and sister, and now Maddie's anger at him. If only things could be simple. He glanced at the pond. The sunlight on the rippling surface bounced back to the underside of the dogwood leaves, making it look as if there were a thousand suns in the sky playing over the tree leaves.

The fountain reminded him of that sheet of music, so he spread the quartered page out on the small table and tried to follow the crabbed notes, but they had no continuity, as he had just demonstrated. And no one could have played such a reach on a pianoforte. As music, they made no sense at all. Perhaps it was some amateur's first composition. In his young days, had he produced such ridiculous flights?

Leighton went back to the puzzle of why it had been sent to him. He could not place the writing, although he was good at that sort of thing. His mind raced back to long sleepless nights spent with Scoville over messages and sheets of decoding. Then he made the sort of leap that usually meant a breakthrough.

The spring in the courtyard had nothing to do with music, but he and Maddie both thought so because they had music in common. What if this piece of paper had nothing to do with music either? And he was the link. But between what and what? It was like an equation with no known factors.

He laughed and pushed it aside when the waiter

brought his food. His mind needed work. Into the vacuum of no work he was trying to create some, to knit up a task out of a nonsense shred of paper. But he lived and worked in a world where everything had a purpose. He was not used to having an unknown, a puzzle piece without a puzzle.

He pulled the sheet toward him again. He had no idea of its purpose and why it had been sent to him. The war with France was over. They were negotiating a peace. Of course, the war in America was far from over. But this had nothing to do with the Foreign Office. It was not so mysterious in its requests. Who would have sent him such a thing, if it was not a joke?

****

Maddie was furious, but this time not at Leighton. As she was driven with her luggage in the Haddon coach up the hill, she gave vent to her frustration by ripping up the cordial note Lady Haddon had sent to Patience inviting Maddie to stay with them until mid-August. It was the second time in the space of two weeks she had been packed up and shipped off as though she was a piece of baggage. She reminded herself that she had thought of seeking such a position. Unfortunately, Lady Haddon was not going to pay her for playing companion to Dierdra. Maddie was there strictly as a house guest, but she felt sure she would be expected to work for her keep.

Why had Patience done this to her? They'd been in the Pump Room talking to Mrs. Marsden, the grandmother, along with Lady Haddon and her daughter. Maddie had felt obliged to chat with Dierdra, though the girl bubbled far too much to suit her. But then Dierdra was several years her junior. Suddenly Patience, who had been in a brown study ever since the post had arrived, got the brilliant notion of farming her out to the Haddons.

When they'd returned to Royal Crescent to pack her things, Maddie had accused her sister of conspiring to put her beyond Leighton's reach. Oddly enough, that had seemed to take Patience by surprise. But she had grasped at it as an excuse to send her own sister away. She'd said that if Leighton really wanted her, Marsden House would be no bar to him.

Now that Lady Haddon's note had been reduced to a pile of very tiny pieces of paper, Maddie did not know what to do with them, so she dropped them into her parasol. What did it all mean? For one thing, the reason she was being sent to the Haddons had nothing to do with Leighton. It was something darker or more serious.

Perhaps their father was coming and Patience wanted her out of the way. No, she would never willingly face him alone. But it would mean Leighton would not be showing up on her doorstep every day, so if their father was coming, Patience could avoid the inevitable scene between the two. Patience could also shift the burden of chaperoning her to someone with more skill at depressing aspirations.

Perhaps that was it. As for what Leighton would do, this was a good test of his ingenuity. As an earl, he could probably get an entree into the house of a mere knight, even though Sir Phillip Haddon was a wealthy and important one. But she rather thought Leighton would not take the easy road. If it was in her power, she meant to see to it that he could not. He should pay for being so secretive. He had never really properly courted her. Now he would have to. She dismissed the truth that her father would never have permitted a normal courtship. It would be interesting to see how long it would take Leighton to breach the fortress of Marsden House, the grandmother's grim four-story edifice that overlooked Bath from the north.

She plastered a polite smile to her face as they approached the walled and gated estate. Yes, it would be interesting to see what Leighton contrived.

****

Leighton was kept waiting in the hall at 6 Royal Crescent. He heard a man and a woman talking with Patience and expected them to still be there as she admitted him. But when Leighton was shown into the morning room, Patience was alone. That gave him an uneasy feeling. Certainly her other company could have left through the adjoining room that gave on to the hallway, but why would they sneak out?

"Where is Maddie?"

Patience looked up at him with a challenge. "Not here, obviously."

"But you said I could call on her here."

"Circumstances have changed."

Leighton parked himself on the sofa without being invited. "What circumstances?"

"I have found Maddie a position. It is a genteel—"

"What?" He leaped to his feet again. "But we are going to be married. She does not need to go into service. Where is she?"

"Papa wanted me to find her a situation, and I have," she said with a satisfied smile.

"And where is that?"

Patience glanced toward a set of double doors. Leighton almost went to thrust them open, for he now suspected Vicar Westlake was behind them. But he restrained himself. What good would that confrontation do?

"So I have to hunt her down again. If you think to throw a rub in the way of our marriage…"

"No, why should I?" She scribbled something on a piece of paper. "What you and Maddie do is no concern of mine, so long as you do not create a scandal."

"But you try to put her beyond my reach."

"How so? Of course, you may be denied when you ask to see her."

"Just what sort of position is this?" He was looming over her now, but Patience showed not the slightest discomfort at his anger.

"A companion, but to a most genteel family."

"Poor Maddie. She is ever taking care of the aged."

"You mistake. She is to keep company with Mrs. Marsden's granddaughter."

"*Where?*" Leighton demanded.

Patience cringed. "No need to shout. At Marsden House. It sits by itself on Richmond Hill. Here, I have drawn you a map."

He took the paper suspiciously. "You had better be telling me true, Patience."

"Why would I lie to you?"

"I think your father might compel you to do many bad things, just because you are afraid of him."

"I am not afraid of Papa. Did I not run away and get married?"

"Did you? I thought he approved."

"Do you think I care what tale he told, once I was free of him? Now go to Maddie and leave me alone." She glanced at the double doors again.

"But we have not finished our visit yet," Leighton

said by way of baiting her.

"We most certainly have." She stood and showed him the door into the hall herself. If Patience was not acting for her father, then Leighton could think of only one reason she would want to be rid of both Maddie and him. She must have a lover. The notion caught him so unexpectedly that a chuckle burst out of him—which he was able to disguise as a coughing fit.

On his way out, he wondered if there was any way he should feel responsible for this childhood friend. She was a grown woman, a widow who should be able to handle her own affairs, whatever they were.

He had never thought Patience's intellect superior, but he had never had cause to doubt her reason before. To carry on a clandestine affair in London was difficult enough. To try to do so in Bath was social suicide.

He stood outside the house a moment, getting his bearings and wondering whether to present himself at Marsden House immediately or to catch Maddie in the Pump Room. He heard Patience talking to someone, and the lower tones of a man's voice. For a moment he thought there was something familiar about it, but it was definitely not Vicar Westlake.

Leighton left Royal Crescent and started uphill, but he had no idea how he was going to gain admission to Marsden House. What he needed was some advice and coaching in the social graces as they pertained to Bath. It was casual here, but would he be allowed to call on Maddie in the family drawing room, or need he go around to the kitchen? If Patience had set this family up as chaperones for Maddie, most likely he would not be admitted at all.

He reversed his steps and headed down the hill. The

only person he knew in Bath who might help him was Dr. Murray, and at this time of day he should be in the Pump Room looking for patients.

Leighton was not disappointed. He spotted the doctor among a crowd of women. To his distress, the doctor introduced him as a young man with an interesting cough. Finally Leighton was able to drag the man away.

"What troubles you?" Murray asked.

"Maddie's sister has placed her with Mrs. Marsden as a companion to her granddaughter Dierdra. I need a way into their house."

"There I can help you. The grandmother is a patient of mine. You have only to return here at four o'clock and I will make you known to each other. But do you really think it will help?"

"What do you mean?"

"The last time you and Miss Westlake talked, you seemed to be at loggerheads."

"Pay that no mind. Maddie will forgive me if I admit my fault, but I must make a chance to speak with her."

"How will it serve to get an introduction to her hostess? They will not let a young woman in their charge go wandering about on her own. You would be better advised to attend the subscription balls they hold twice a week in the Upper Assembly Rooms."

"But if I am running tame in their house, I know I will be able to get back in Maddie's good graces."

"Seems like a crack-brained idea to me, but—oh, well, the course of true love…" Murray shrugged.

"See you at four o'clock."

****

Leighton spent the afternoon getting acquainted

with the rest of the streets in Bath. Within a few hours he had a reliable mental map of the place. Once he saw a tall man who looked so familiar from the back he felt compelled to follow him, but he lost him in a side street. Most likely it was someone he had known in Spain but just could not place. Since the doctor was here, the city might very well be crawling with veterans.

He shrugged off the feeling that someone was watching him. London was large and anonymous. In a place as small as Bath, you were likely to keep seeing the same faces over and over. And the stream of shoppers and saunterers crowding the streets was probably normal traffic for the town.

After changing his shirt, cravat, and coat, he returned to the Pump Room. There was a surprising number of dandies there, besides ladies both old and young, but no doctor. Leighton gave a sigh of impatience, had another coughing fit, and was just recovering himself when an older lady in a gray walking dress cast him a concerned look.

"Are you all right, young man?"

"Oh, fine. I was walking too fast, I suppose. I was to meet Dr. Murray here."

"I know the man well. He is my physician—"

A burst of laughter from the dandy set who crowded around the younger women interrupted her.

"Popinjays!"

"I beg your pardon."

"Them, not you. They are just waiting about to pounce on Dierdra when she gets here. Fortune hunters and ne'er-do-wells, the lot of them."

"Even the captain?" Leighton asked, nodding toward the tall Horse Guards officer who looked so magnificent.

"A half-pay officer, no doubt."

"But why would they pounce on your Dierdra?"

"She's an innocent. But no more of that. Her maid has never been able to fend them off, but I lay odds Miss Westlake will give them their marching orders."

"Oh, you must be…Lady Haddon." He conferred the mother's title on her rather than the grandmother's, forming what he thought was a clever plan. He bowed and smugly wondered if he would be able to do without the doctor's introduction. "I am sure you are right. Let me introduce myself. I am Leighton Stone."

"What makes you say that about Miss Westlake?" The woman fluttered her fan in front of her breast as she looked him over.

"I am somewhat acquainted with Miss Westlake. I feel confident you are right about her keeping men at bay."

Suddenly she laughed and cuffed him with her fan. "You think I am Dierdra's mother?"

"Aren't you?" Leighton stepped back and regarded her. She was stately and dignified and there were a few strands of silver in her fine brown hair.

"Lord, no. I am her grandmother."

"Grandmother?" Leighton feigned surprise. "No, I am sorry, madam. I will allow you to be her mother but never her grandmother, unless you had her mother when you were but a child yourself."

"Flatterer," she said with a becoming flush. "Here they come now. Lay you odds they can't even get across the room without being stopped."

Leighton glanced at the granddaughter, stunning in yellow poplin, her gold ringlets bouncing. Maddie, carrying a large shopping basket full of packages, walked beside Dierdra, trying to persuade her of something.

"Of the Bedford Stones?" the grandmother asked.

The girls had been swallowed up by a crowd of five gentlemen. He supposed he would have to go get them.

Leighton turned, puzzled. "Bedford? Oh, you mean my family. No, Hereford. Shall I bring the girls to you?"

"Do you think you can?" she challenged.

Leighton chuckled. "I think I can contrive something, if you will oblige me by having a seat." He led Mrs. Marsden to a chair, then started across the room but glanced back.

She perched on the seat provided but did not look particularly helpless as she scowled at the crowd of men.

Leighton made fanning motions at her.

She gave him a puzzled look but complied by fluttering her fan as he strode across the room.

Maddie was doing her best to disentangle the flirtatious Dierdra from the gaggle of men while nearly half the compliments were flying in her direction. To make matters worse, there was Leighton coming up to her. If he made a jealous scene, she would never forgive him.

"Excuse me, Miss Haddon. Your grandmother seems to be feeling unwell. Would you come to her?"

"Grandmother? She is never ill."

Maddie didn't like the way Dierdra looked Leighton up and down, nor the way she let him take her arm and lead her away. What the devil was he playing at? She dismissed the rest of the men with a glare and trailed after Leighton and Dierdra, failing to catch whatever words of flattery he was pouring into her ears.

"By the way, I am Leighton Stone."

"I'm Dierdra Haddon, Sir Phillip Haddon's daughter."

"Yes, I know."

"Grandmother, what is it? Are you all right?"

"Perfectly. Are you finished making a spectacle of yourself?"

"Well, I cannot be rude to people, can I? You do look flushed. Perhaps Mr. Stone should call you a chair."

"Certainly not!"

"How do you come to know Mister Stone?" Dierdra asked.

"Chance met. But he is acquainted with Miss Westlake."

Maddie felt her cheeks flush for no reason other than anger. Bad enough she was sold into service to the Haddons, but it was the outside of enough to have to be polite to Leighton when it was probably all his fault.

"Yes, Leighton and I have known each other for ages." Maddie realized some further explanation of their connection was necessary, for Dierdra was already looking at Leighton far too greedily. Maddie decided she would not lose her earl without a fight, even though she was feeling out of charity with him at the moment. "We played together."

"You grew up together?" Dierdra asked.

"We played music together," Leighton corrected. "I am in her father's parish, and since she was the only *child* in the district with any faculty for an instrument, the burden of church programs fell to us."

"Ah, I see. You were her music master," Dierdra's grandmother said.

"No—yes," Maddie said in quick succession. If

Leighton did not blab about being an earl, she might be willing to let him lord it over her as far as music went.

"Well, which is it?" Dierdra said, a pouted frown marring her mouth.

Leighton gave a cough. "Not officially her music master. I may have taught her a little of what I learned at university, but Maddie has a natural ear. She is as good at the pianoforte as I am. We play duets sometimes, or I accompany her on the cello."

Leighton smiled at Maddie, and her heart melted. How could she have doubted him? To be sure, he had inflicted himself on Dierdra's grandmother only in order to talk to her.

"Leighton composes too," she said, seeking to further obscure his identity.

"Indeed?" Mrs. Marsden said, eyeing him with new respect.

"For my own amusement, though we have performed some of my music at the church."

Dierdra eyed him with wonder. "I have never met a composer before."

Leighton could not avoid the chuckle and the inevitable coughing fit that followed.

Dr. Murray strode over to them. "I see you've met my new patient." He pounded Leighton on the back. "Sorry I am late, lad. I had an emergency."

"Indeed," Leighton croaked.

"Well, it was not me taking up your time with silly illnesses," the older woman said. "Will you do us the pleasure of dining with us before the subscription ball tomorrow night, Doctor?"

"Why, thank you, but Leighton and I had planned to dine together."

Maddie saw the doctor wink at Leighton. Her betrothed put on his most innocent face.

"Oh, go ahead, Murray. We can delay our dinner."

"Grandmother, why cannot Leighton dine with us as well?"

"My dear girl, I do not even know your parents," Leighton said. "A very odd start they would think it."

"Nonsense," Mrs. Marsden replied. "The house in Bath is my home, not my son-in law's. Of course you may dine with us since I am inviting you."

"I would be delighted," Leighton said with a bow.

"And Dr. Murray, bring that nice Lieutenant Reid with you. So refined and polite. Now we must return home or we shall be late for tonight's dinner."

"We'll walk with you," Leighton offered, taking Mrs. Marsden's arm.

"With that terrible cough?" Maddie gibed.

"Oh, I think the reason Bath is so famous for its cures has nothing to do with the waters but with making invalids walk up all these hills. I assure you I have vastly improved in the few days I have been here."

To Maddie's surprise, Leighton took the basket of shopping from her and walked with Mrs. Marsden. The doctor got between Maddie and Dierdra.

"Are you going to the ball tomorrow night?" Murray asked Maddie.

"Oh, I do not think so."

"Of course you must attend," Dierdra said. "It is so much more fun when one has a best friend to confide in. You can wear your new dress, the white one."

The doctor nodded. "Things are rather informal here in Bath. You will enjoy yourself very much."

When they reached Marsden House, Maddie

thought Leighton might have tried harder to get a word alone with her, but instead he left with the doctor without even entering the house. What was he playing at? And why in God's name had she introduced him as a music instructor? She hated to think what Mrs. Marsden or Lady Haddon would say when they found out who he really was. But actually she had told no untruth. She merely had not puffed off Leighton's consequence, and he had looked as though he enjoyed the joke. She wondered what Patience would say if she knew how easily Leighton had breached the walls of Marsden House.

****

"Well, does that make up for my tardiness?" the doctor asked him on the way back to the hotel.

"I am amazed. Dinner and the ball. Surely I will find ample opportunity to woo the reluctant Maddie."

"And she did not seem badly disposed toward you. Did you buy a subscription to the balls?"

"Yes, and found out where I can obtain a license. In two weeks we can be married and no one will be able to stop us."

"You know, if you were a conniving fellow, you could probably have the lovely Dierdra and all her fortune."

"She has a fortune?"

"Yes, she's a considerable heiress and no siblings to share with."

"Poor girl."

"Why do you say that?"

"Maddie must know my interest is genuine, since she has no fortune, but Dierdra will never be able to tell when she is being preyed upon."

"Yes, that is why they watch her so closely. But there are fellows who would take Maddie just for her looks."

"I must remember she is not safe here either."

Leighton dined with the doctor again, this time in the main dining room at the hotel. They were joined by Lieutenant Reid, a limping soldier in the uniform of a cavalry officer, whom Leighton assumed to be one of the doctor's patients. Leighton had also seen him around the city, but if Reid had noticed him in the Peninsula he did not speak of it. He showed no surprise at the dinner invitation to Marsden House and seemed content to listen to Leighton's questions for the doctor about Bath and the balls.

"They are held twice a week, Monday and Thursday. Sometimes there is a theme, such as costumes, but not tomorrow."

"Is evening dress appropriate?

"Yes, or military uniforms."

Reid nodded.

"Do you both go?" Leighton asked.

"Yes, I shall look in on it," the doctor said.

Reid shrugged. "I shan't be dancing for a while, but more goes on at a ball than dancing."

Leighton nodded, trying not to put a grim twist on the man's words, but Reid never smiled. Though his speech gave Leighton no reason to distrust him, there was an unexplained reserve about Reid that made Leighton think the man was studying him.

Then it hit him that Reid was probably in pain. While Leighton had come home with no more than a scar, Reid must have taken a career-ending wound. Leighton tried to think of some way to make it up to him, as though it was his fault. Then he stopped and scolded himself for assuming Reid could not manage on his own. He was always doing that, taking over and finding solutions where others did not even perceive there to be a problem.

Instead, he should be applying himself to the problem of how to court Maddie. He must start with an apology, then engage her interest, possibly by showing her that mysterious piece of sheet music. Now there was a puzzle. Perhaps, if he could get a moment alone with Maddie, she would have some idea what it could mean.

Chapter Eleven

Leighton returned from his ride on Jasper the next day to discover Tibbs out and his rooms in obvious disorder, worse even than he usually left them. But when he looked through his baggage, the only thing that seemed to be missing was the packet of music that had been delivered the day before.

He was just hanging up one or two of his coats when Tibbs returned.

"Well, really now, if you couldn't find something, I think you might have waited for me to get back."

"I didn't do this. The door was unlocked and clothes scattered all over," Leighton protested.

"You expect me to believe that? You were looking for something and made your usual mess."

"You must have left the door unlocked. It's a good thing I had all my cash with me, or we would have been robbed."

"Give me that!" Tibbs snatched a handful of neckcloths from Leighton and went off toward the bedchamber grumbling.

Leighton sat in defeat at the small writing desk and pulled out of his wallet the piece of music he had been writing for Maddie. The folded-up page of strange handwritten music fell out. For the first time he realized it had a scent to it. Not a perfume but something stronger. Tea, or…tobacco. That was it. The paper smelled like tobacco. So what did that do for him, except to bring back memories of his father chuckling as he filled his pipe?

He had always found time to listen to Leighton, no matter what crack-brained scheme he had in mind. He had let Leighton try some of his ideas for repairing buildings or creating better farming implements. Sometimes these had even worked, and his father's praise had been effusive. It had almost compensated for his mother's ridicule. How odd that they had married. They were nothing alike, not like him and Maddie. *They* were made for each other.

He called back the simple melody of the fountain in the courtyard and sat writing until he had finished the piece. Of course, he would not know what it sounded like until he had access to a pianoforte.

"Tibbs?" He had forgotten the man was angry at him. Would he even reply?

"What now?" Tibbs poked his head around the door frame.

"Is there a piano here in the hotel?"

"What the devil do you want with a piano? You said you have one at your estate."

"But I need one now— Oh, never mind."

Tibbs stalked away. "Wants a piano one minute, then it's never mind."

"God, look at the time. Have you pressed my evening clothes as I asked?" When Leighton pursued him to the bedroom, he found Tibbs looking heavenward and shaking his head. But his black swallowtail coat and knee breeches were laid out on the bed.

****

Maddie looked at Dierdra primping in the mirror

and wondered why she did not envy the girl. Dierdra had beauty, wealth, and doting parents. Maddie had not met Sir Phillip Haddon yet. He would not arrive from London until the next day. But tonight Dierdra seemed brittle and unsteady, for all her gaiety.

She looked up at Maddie. "You said you grew up with Leighton. Is he like a brother to you?"

"I think I used to feel that way about him, since I had no brothers of my own. His sisters and he were always at the parsonage. They took lessons from my father."

"Good."

Maddie was still puzzling over the comment when Lady Haddon looked in on them. "You are lovely, both of you. Remember now, this is a practice field for London. You cannot afford to disgrace yourself here, Dierdra. Madeline, your hair is enchanting. Simple, yet elegant. Show Dierdra's maid how to do hers like that for tomorrow."

Maddie nodded, knowing the door would close again before she had a chance to reply. Lady Haddon reminded her a little of Leighton's mother, and she wondered what it would be like to live at Longbridge. Perhaps she could not handle his mother and would feel like a servant there as well. She heard the piano distantly through the oak door.

Dierdra looked up at her. "Who could be playing?"

"Leighton must be here." At the same time Maddie damned him for his arrogance, she followed the tune with her mind and had to admit he was good. She hurried back to her room for her shawl but reminded herself not to rush down the stairs just because he had arrived.

The piano had been too tempting. When shown into

the empty salon, Leighton had immediately sat down and started picking out the notes of the song he was writing. He got out a pencil stub to make a correction midway, then made it to the end of the piece, sitting back to think about Maddie and how he would play it for her.

The sound of one person clapping caused him to look around in puzzlement.

"You must be Mr. Stone." The woman who approached was ramrod-straight, with golden hair, and bore some slight resemblance to Dierdra. She reminded Leighton of the room, so precise with every last bit of lace perfect. Such a woman would want to put him in his place immediately.

"I'm so sorry," Leighton said as he rose and bowed. "About the piano, I mean. I should have asked first."

"Nonsense. You did no harm. Please sit."

"I am Leighton Stone."

"So I surmised. I am Lady Haddon. Do you make a long stay in Bath?"

"My plans are indefinite."

"Indeed."

Leighton caught the disapproval and guessed the cause—Dierdra. A wary mother would always try to keep ineligible men away from her daughter. Leighton was not in the habit of being disapproved of, and it amused him. "Do you make a long stay in Bath?" he countered, prompting a look of surprise from her.

"My mother lives here. We return to the country again in August."

"Ah, grouse."

"Yes, though my husband is the only one who hunts."

She was probably worried she might have to

entertain him again, might even be cornered into having him at the estate. Leighton knew how to be disarming. A frontal attack always worked. He sent his hostess a searching look. "I'm sure I have offended you somehow. If it was not the piano, then I cannot make out what I have said or done to put you out."

She looked surprised but not shocked. "I am sure there is nothing offensive in your speech or manners. Certainly your playing was wonderful."

"Oh, I see. You just don't like me."

She hesitated with her mouth open and blinked at him. "In a word, no." She delivered her most quelling stare.

Leighton smiled brilliantly and nodded as though pleased with himself for having solved the puzzle. "I thought so."

"Don't you want to know why?"

"Oh, please don't tell me. Ten to one it is something I cannot mend anyway."

Leighton sat at the piano again and began to run over the melody to Maddie's song as though he did not care at all for Lady Haddon's opinion of him, which was exactly the case.

She moved around to the side of the grand piano.

When he saw her standing there, he stopped playing.

"I tell you to your face I do not like you and you seem delighted. What sort of man are you?"

"An ordinary one, I think. But you are such a rare woman. Don't you see how you intrigue me? Think how dull conversation would be if we all liked each other. I look forward to becoming the best of enemies with you."

She laughed. With her guard down she suddenly looked more like her daughter. "You are the oddest boy.

After this dinner and ball I shall have no more to do with you."

She was flirting with him. "Yes, that is by far the best plan for you. But on the other hand, I do play well, so I could be of some use to a hostess who wanted to get up a musical entertainment."

"I have no such intention."

He hesitated and looked up at her. "I think your mother might. Why else would she have invited me?"

"Why else, indeed? Let me make myself perfectly clear. My daughter is destined to marry well."

Leighton thought his puzzled look genuine enough. "How does Dierdra come into it?"

"I am merely stating that I have no intention of letting her throw herself away on a music master."

Leighton laughed. "Is that what you were worried about?" He was trying to think of a way to assuage her fears without giving away his real purpose when her mother came in and demanded to hear again the piece he had been playing. By the time he had finished, Maddie and Dierdra were there as well. It was not how he had planned to present the piece to Maddie, and he felt that it had been cheapened by his playing it for someone else first.

"Mr. Stone is a music instructor, Cora," Mrs. Marsden said. "I thought while he is in town, he could give Dierdra a few lessons."

Leighton could see the objection rising to Lady Haddon's face and interrupted, "But I am here on holiday."

"I thought you were here to recover from your cold," Mrs. Marsden replied.

"That too, but I don't think I will have time to give

any serious instruction."

"Nonsense. Dierdra already knows how to play. You will have time to make some progress with her if you come every other day."

Maddie glared at Leighton as if to say, "Now see what you've gotten yourself into." But he decided it served his purpose. The more he was in the house, the more chance to see Maddie.

"I shall do my best, but does Dierdra even want piano lessons?" He looked toward the excited girl, who was twining her fingers together.

"Oh, above all things," Dierdra agreed, thus stopping her mother from vetoing the idea.

Dr. Murray made his usual timely entrance and presented Lieutenant Reid, who had not met Lady Haddon before. Leighton was pleased to note that she scowled at the soldier as blackly as she had at Leighton, and also that the man did no more than blink at her rudeness.

"Well, we are only waiting for Gifford," the grandmother said, drumming her fingers on the arm of her chair. "John Gifford is Sir Phillip's cousin," she said ominously.

She did not say "and heir," but why else would a cousin be running tame in the house. Leighton thought perhaps he was also the man chosen for Dierdra to marry. There was no title to pass on and whether the estate was entailed to male kin only was immaterial. They wanted to make sure the fortune Dierdra inherited stayed in the family.

Gifford came into the room looking like a smaller edition of the Prince Regent, whom Leighton was sure he meant to copy. Leighton could have sworn his late appearance was intentional, an entrance to add to his consequence. After he was introduced to everyone and had scowled at both Leighton and Reid in a good imitation of Dierdra's mother, he took Dierdra's arm as though claiming her and waited for the others to precede him into the dining room. Dr. Murray took that as his cue to raise Mrs. Marsden to her feet and escort her. Reid moved toward Maddie without even thinking about it. Leighton now had no choice but to take Lady Haddon's arm to lead her in to dinner.

"Understand me, Stone," she said through gritted teeth. "These lessons will be strictly chaperoned by Miss Westlake. Do I make myself clear?"

"Absolutely."

In the loose protocol that covered the situation, a lieutenant clearly was more important than a music master. But Reid had automatically offered to escort a woman of lesser station by assuming Leighton would lead in the highest ranking woman present. Either Reid was not a lieutenant or he knew that Leighton had a title. How? Possibly from Dr. Murray, or even from his own observations in the Peninsula, though Leighton always went by Mr. Stone there.

If he was puzzled, so was Lady Haddon. She was also discontented with the seating arrangement, which placed Dierdra between Leighton and Reid. He asked himself who could have contrived that, and Dierdra smiled smugly at him.

Some look, almost a reprimand, passed from Murray to Reid, as though he was being admonished for his mistake. There was something more to the connection between these two than doctor and patient. That was another little puzzle Leighton would have to solve when he had a moment.

One black look from Gifford and suddenly Leighton knew why he had been invited by the grandmother. Probably Reid was there to annoy Gifford, as well. Grandmother did not like the heir apparent, and Leighton was inclined to agree with her assessment.

One reason became clear even before the first course was served. Gifford interrupted. Every time Mrs. Marsden said something, he either finished her sentence or countered it with his own opinion before she had finished speaking. As Leighton sipped his soup, he traded looks with Maddie. She gave him a dry smile that indicated Gifford normally behaved this way. The grandmother bore it with resignation. When Dierdra's mother spoke, Gifford fell over himself agreeing with her. The word "sycophant" came to mind. If Lady Haddon was this easily flattered, it meant Leighton could get away with anything, but it also meant Dierdra would be marrying a fool.

By the removal of the first course, even Dierdra was getting tired of having her lines trampled upon and she simply quit saying anything. Maddie sent her a sad smile that made Dierdra blush. Whatever Leighton did, he should make a push to show up Gifford for what he was.

There he went, interfering again. But perhaps he and Maddie between them could think of some way to spring the girl from this trap.

"I suppose you saw a bit of action in the Peninsula," Gifford said to Reid when the table had been silenced by his overbearing rudeness.

Reid slowly took a sip of wine, waiting to see if an answer was expected. "Yes. I was attached to Lord Wellington's staff, so I was in more than a few battles."

Wellington's staff, Leighton thought. Yet he had never seen him. Perhaps Reid was one of the observing officers, spending all his time in the field.

Gifford motioned for a servant to refill his goblet and took a large gulp before he proceeded with the interrogation. "Where did you take your wound?"

"Albuera," Reid answered.

"I haven't heard—" Gifford started before Reid had finished.

"Salamanca, Vitoria, and finally Toulouse," the lieutenant finished.

"How terrible," Dierdra said, casting a worshipful look at the soldier.

"How very unlucky," Gifford corrected, "to have your career shattered in such a way."

Reid sent him that calculating look. "Fortunately, I have an estate to return to and a title someday. Many have no expectations, now that the war is over."

Suddenly Dierdra's mother looked at Reid with interest.

"Lieutenant Reid's father is Lord Thorpe," Mrs. Marsden said.

There was dead silence for a moment as Gifford fumed and Dierdra's mother ran over the Thorpe holdings in her mind. Leighton felt someone had to say something and was just about to.

"But the war isn't over," Maddie said, "not the one with America. Will you be spared that, at least?"

"I doubt I will be recovered enough to go before a peace has been negotiated. I hear that the Russian emperor is brokering a treaty, and that the American ambassadors are already in St. Petersburg."

"So trade may soon resume unfettered," Leighton

concluded. "That is good to know."

Both Murray and Reid seemed to be watching him to see how news of the peace would take him. Now, why was that?

"Are you concerned with international trade, Mr. Stone?" Gifford asked.

"Why, no, we barely— That is, with the poor harvest, British farms can barely feed the populace. There's little in the way of foodstuffs for export. Though I imagine the manufacturers and ship owners will breathe a sigh of relief."

"Ladies, shall we leave the gentlemen to their port?" Mrs. Marsden said as she rose. "Keep in mind, Gifford, that we mean to go out tonight."

Maddie left with a resigned look, but Gifford looked positively rebellious. After the decanter was passed, Leighton found himself wondering if the man behaved any better when Sir Phillip was present. Probably he fawned on him as well as on his wife.

Reid excused himself to go into the garden and smoke a cigar. Leighton wished he had acquired the habit, if for no other reason than to escape Gifford's pompous monologue on the rudeness of Dierdra's grandmother.

"Well, it *is* her house," Leighton said.

The man glared at him. "For the moment," Gifford replied as though he planned to murder her in her sleep.

"And that Westlake girl. What is she doing here?"

"A companion for Dierdra, who seems to lack friends."

"Encroaching—"

"That is quite enough," Leighton said in a voice he scarcely ever used, unless he was reprimanding a fractious colt. He stood. "A *gentleman* does not gossip about guests, especially when they are not his own. I shall see you downstairs, Doctor."

As Leighton exited, he heard only, "What the devil?" from Gifford, then Murray murmuring some soothing words. Perhaps being a music master in the house would strain his acting abilities more than he had thought. He could see himself planting his fist in Gifford's face before many days had elapsed.

Chapter Twelve

Instead of going to the drawing room, Maddie went upstairs to get her fan. Dierdra popped into her room.

"Isn't Mr. Stone handsome and Lieutenant Reid brave?" The girl collapsed on Maddie's bed with a sigh.

Maddie found herself smiling at Dierdra's immaturity. "Which do you like better?" she asked.

"Both of them. I cannot decide."

"But you won't be allowed to decide, will you?"

Dierdra sat up, the dreamy glitter gone from her eyes. "No, Mama wants me to marry Gifford. He is such a boor."

"What if you refuse?"

"I can't do that," Dierdra said with a pathetic look. "Can I?"

"You could refuse him, but not in a bout of tears. You would have to use logic. Point out what an embarrassment he is."

"I can't call up logic, and all argument deserts me when Papa is shouting at me."

"I know what you mean, but if your papa talks as much as mine, you have plenty of time to order your argument while he is chewing at you."

"He interrupts like Gifford."

"Then this will annoy him. When he interrupts, ask politely if you may please finish your sentence."

"I could never dare do that to Papa."

"Well, practice on Gifford."

When they finally assembled in the hall, the gentlemen set out to walk to the assembly rooms, except for Gifford. He crowded Maddie and Dierdra on one bench of the carriage, where they sat opposite the two older ladies. Maddie thought it would have been handsome of Gifford to give his seat to Reid, whose limp could not possibly be improved by the hike down the hill, but she kept her peace about that. The carriage arrived before the gentlemen, so Maddie suggested the ladies wait for them in the anteroom. But Lady Haddon was too busy sizing up the occupants of the salons to notice. She moved forward to greet a distinguished gentleman.

"Oh, good. Gifford's gone to the card room," Dierdra said. "That's a blessing. No broken feet for the ladies tonight."

Maddie and the grandmother laughed. Maddie hoped that Mrs. Marsden would not let Dierdra's parents force her into a match with the self-centered young man who had just abandoned them.

When the gentlemen arrived, Leighton followed Mrs. Marsden and the girls to the dowager's corner. Dierdra's grandmother introduced the party, and Leighton delighted even the oldest ladies by insisting they should be dancing. Maddie sent him a rueful smile. He knew from experience that it took only a few compliments and jokes to get the goodwill of these senior ladies. Though several blushed and furled their fans, none accepted his invitation to dance, so he, Dr. Murray, Dierdra, and Maddie joined a set that was forming near their end of the room. Reid had somehow disappeared.

Murray was a graceful dancer for such a big man.

He never lost his place and was able to cover for any gaffe Dierdra made. When it was time for Leighton and Maddie to go down the line, Leighton stole the moment to say, "Can you forgive me?"

Instead of saying, "For what?" as he had no doubt expected, she replied, "Which of your sins did you have in mind?"

She was joking, of course, but his thoughtfulness for the rest of the set made her feel sorry for him. Here he was ready to apologize and she was acting like a spoiled miss. If she had been an easy conquest for Leighton, that was because she did love him. She should forgive him with a good grace rather than torture him.

When the set ended, she walked with him toward the tea table.

"I suppose I am in worse trouble than I thought." He handed her a cup. "Could you speed things up by reading me a catalogue of my sins?"

"Very well. Are we speaking of you ignoring me in the Pump Room, your intrusion into Marsden House, your inattention at dinner, or your keeping from me the fact that your life has been in constant danger these past six years?" She delivered this with a prim smile, but Leighton was taking it all seriously.

"As for the first three, I am playing a role. If I spend all my moments mooning over you, Lady Haddon will get suspicious and tell Patience I am here." He picked up a cup of tea himself and almost choked on the bitterness.

Maddie pursed her lips. "As I am sure you have guessed, it is ultimately your fault I have been dumped at Marsden House." She watched over the rim of her teacup what the addition of this crime would do to him. He got a wild, puzzled look in his eyes.

126

"I had not thought Patience absolutely against my suit."

"I think there is more to it than that. She is perfectly able to cope with you, but Papa may be coming." As this sank in, Maddie studied his finely chiseled face, browned she now realized from his time in Spain. She could understand Dierdra's fascination.

"Because she wrote to him?" He looked intense in the stark white shirt and black coat.

"Be serious, Leighton. Would anyone willingly bring Papa down on herself for a visit?"

He wiped one hand across his forehead. "Good point. Of course not. But he might come here to check up on you. By putting you beyond my reach, she also keeps him away from you."

"And perhaps she knew you would get an entree to Marsden House." She set down her cup. "She is on to your clever wiles."

"I do not feel very clever. I see now how I have neglected you. Are you absolutely finished with me, or will you forgive me all these things?"

She studied his dear face full of abject worry. "Yes, of course."

"Uh…"

"Of course I forgive you, even for not sharing the danger with me during the war."

He breathed a sigh of relief and got rid of the teacup. "I need time to explain that. The piano lesson is scheduled for three o'clock tomorrow. If you came down early, we might be able to—"

"What are you two doing?" Mrs. Hadden asked. "You are going to miss the next set."

Maddie had not danced so much in years, not since

she and Leighton had taken turns playing for both their sisters to learn the steps. Those had been merry parties, with the vicar never knowing the purpose. Maddie had been a child then, but she still remembered the feel of Leighton's hands, so strong and competent, and she went through the steps of the country dance as easily as though she had done it every day since.

By the end of the second set of dances, the room had heated up.

"Let me get you something cool to drink this time," Leighton suggested.

While he went for cups of punch, Maddie noticed Lady Haddon watching him with a puzzled frown. Leighton began to laugh when he got back to her.

"What is so funny?" she asked as he handed her the cup.

"Lady Haddon seemed to think I meant to ravish her daughter, so she cannot figure out why I have not even partnered her."

"Dierdra has every young man in the room panting after her. Besides, with that innocent air of yours, no one would suspect you of having designs on anyone."

"Thanks—I think. So Patience wasn't at all worried about us eloping."

"I told you, she may have heard from Papa. She did get a letter and was so adamant I come here that I…gave in."

"Just like you gave in to your father."

She took a step back from him. "Which does not mean I cannot think for myself or make a plan on my own. I had to trick him many times just to take care of your tenants."

"I realize that now. I am going to figure out what

Patience is up to. Even though I have not the slightest wish to call on her tomorrow, I will do so anyway, at the usual time."

Maddie thought for a moment. "Perhaps Dierdra and I should call too. In some ways, this situation could make it easier for us to meet, now that I have decided I want to talk to you."

"Maddie, I swear, I would have told you about my work if I could have."

"You did not trust me," she whispered.

"That's not true. It was the post I did not trust. That's why I had to go to Spain in the first place. Too many of Wellington's dispatches home were getting opened. The French always knew our plans, those first few years."

"Really? In that case, I truly do forgive you. But do not let it happen again."

"I should hope not. An entire war?" Leighton tossed his punch off in one gulp, then gave a cough. "Are you sure you want to go to Patience's house? I don't think they will let you two go alone, and you might meet your father there."

"You think I do not have the courage to face him, but I do."

"What are you two chatting about?" Dierdra's grandmother demanded. "You missed getting a place in the next set."

"It's his lungs," Maddie lied. "He isn't sure so much dancing is good for him."

When Maddie elbowed Leighton in the side, he produced another creditable cough. Lady Marsden left them with a curt nod and an admonition to rest himself.

"That was close," Maddie said, as she watched Leighton feeling his side.

"I'll say. You almost broke my rib."

"Don't be an idiot. What do we do now?"

"Hold out for two more weeks. By then you will be twenty-one and we can get married without anyone's permission."

"Do you think you can stay out of trouble that long?"

"Maddie, this is Bath, an old woman's town. Other than having my room plundered, nothing exciting ever happens."

"I meant stay out of trouble with me. Your room was robbed?"

"No, searched. The only thing taken was a packet of music."

"Oh, come now, who would steal such a thing? You probably mislaid it."

"No, it is gone, except for one sheet. That is what I want to consult you about. Also I have the oddest feeling I've been watched ever since I came into the city."

She stared at him. "But the war in the Peninsula is over. Unless my father hired someone to follow you, I cannot imagine why anyone would spy on you."

"Neither can I."

"You miss it," she accused. "You miss being important and deciphering codes and going to Spain and Portugal."

"I do not. I would far rather be home now rather than having to chase off even to Bath."

"Need I remind you that it is your fault I was shipped off to Bath in the first place?" She thrust the cup into his hand so forcefully he flinched. Then she left him by the potted palm, holding two empty punch cups and biting his lower lip as though he could not figure out why she was upset. She would forgive him again, of course, but if he expected to marry her, he was going to have to stop taking her for granted.

They left the ball when the carriage arrived. The gentlemen did not accompany them but went to their respective hotels, except for Gifford, who had disappeared. On the way home in the carriage, Maddie tried to define what she wanted from Leighton, how she wanted him to treat her. At the same time that she wanted him to flatter her and compliment her as he did other women, she still treasured those moments when they spoke as frankly to each other as though they were still children. She was not sure what she wanted from him, except that she wanted him to herself.

She tossed around in her mind Leighton's suspicion of being watched. True, she had seen Lieutenant Reid observing him from the perimeter of the room, but with his leg, what had he to do but watch people. For all she knew, he might have been watching Dierdra or her. Yet Leighton was usually so sensible, even in his trust of her to take care of things in his stead. Why did she resent that trust? Because he had depended on her for the lesser work and kept for himself the important things, encrypting and decrypting intelligence for the war. He was going to have to take her more seriously from now on.

Chapter Thirteen

The next day, Leighton slept late and missed breakfast. Indeed he woke at all only because Tibbs dropped a boot he'd been polishing. Certainly that had been deliberate, but he was grateful for it. After dressing, he went down to the courtyard with the fountain and had his lunch, then sat enjoying his customary brandy and water as he worked on "Maddie's Song" in the garden. He was adding the left-hand accompaniment and meant to try it out that afternoon when he gave Dierdra her lesson. If he turned up early, she might still be dressing and he would have access to the piano while he waited. So intense was his absorption that when a shadow loomed over his table, without looking for the waiter, he held up his glass. "I'd like another brandy, please."

The glass was silently removed from his hand and deposited on the table without any reply.

Leighton hesitated, then looked up. The tall gray-haired man who glared down at him was a stranger. "I am sorry. I thought you were the waiter." This caused the stiff face above him to turn an alarming shade of red and the salt-and-pepper mustache to bristle.

"Are you Leighton Stone?" a gravelly voice demanded.

"Yes." Leighton stood up. "Do I know you?"

"I believe you are acquainted with my daughter."

"Daughter?"

"I am Sir Phillip Haddon."

"Haddon?" So much for first impressions. But it would not do to be obsequious. "Oh, Mrs. Marsden's son-in-law." Leighton could sense a fuming from the stiff figure.

"Yes, and my wife's husband. But the matter at hand is my daughter."

"I know," Leighton said as though consulting a faulty memory. "Music lessons. I don't think she really has a particle of interest in music lessons, but her grandmother insists."

"And *you* are interested in music."

Leighton could hear the skepticism in his voice and wondered if he dared try to win this lion over. At least he could disarm him. "Of course. Please, have a seat and join me. Do you read music?"

"I—no, I do not. What has that to do with anything?" Haddon remained standing. Of necessity, so did Leighton.

He fell back on his ruse during the Peninsular Wars, that of an obtuse young scholar trying to make what he could of his grand tour with most of the continent in ruins. "I have been torn between an eighth and a sixteenth note for the end of this measure. I suppose you cannot advise me."

"What? No! I do not wish to discuss your music."

"Oh, what did you want?"

"I want to make it abundantly clear that my daughter is off limits."

"Off limits?" Leighton thought he effectively switched his face from an expression of confusion to one of glee. "You mean I don't have to give her music lessons?" The relief in Leighton's voice should have been convincing enough for anyone.

"I mean there is no chance I would ever approve a match between her and—and an itinerant musician."

"Oh, that." Leighton allowed himself a chuckle as he tossed his score onto the table, causing Haddon's complexion to darken even further. "But your wife has already warned me about that. Don't the two of you talk?"

Haddon's eyes bulged as though he wondered if he was dealing with a maniac. "Having Mrs. Haddon say not to concern myself over something causes me to immediately concern myself."

"Well, if you don't want Dierdra to have lessons, I am off the hook."

The man swayed on his feet, looking Leighton up and down and gnawing his lip. "The lessons will be fine, but you are not to be falling in love with her."

"Not likely."

Haddon leaned on the table with both fists curled. "What do you mean by that? Dierdra is the most sought-after heiress in Bath."

Leighton toyed with the notion of resorting to the truth, but he hated to waste it on such an unpromising inquisitor. "My affections are already engaged."

Haddon looked down at the pages of music on the table. "Oh, I see. Your muse."

Leighton thought a moment and nodded vigorously. "If it would make you feel any better, you could stay for the lesson. It won't take above an hour."

The man looked away, then back at Leighton. "We shall see."

After Haddon stalked away, Leighton expelled an anxious breath and sat down. He closed his eyes for a moment and took out his handkerchief to mop his brow. The salon was likely to be a bit crowded this afternoon. That did not bode well for having any private conversation with Maddie. And, he recalled, she was angry with him again. What was that about? What a fool he was. How could courting one woman have gotten so complicated?

****

Leighton wondered if Maddie was angry enough not keep her appointment to call on her sister. But at one o'clock he called on Patience, and Maddie was there with Dierdra. It was a stilted visit, no one being able to say anything to the point because of Dierdra's presence.

It was during one of the awkward pauses that he figured out what he'd said wrong last night. He had made it sound as though coming to Bath for Maddie was a bother, when it was the most important thing in his life. Anything else he did, even his work during the war, should never have been as important as Maddie. But he was fighting an uphill battle to convince her of that now.

Throughout the half hour, Leighton had again the distinct feeling that he was being watched. It was a relief when the girls took their leave. An unexpected benefit was being able to walk them to Marsden Hall.

"What did you say to Father?" Dierdra demanded. "He came home raging about you."

Leighton grimaced. "Oh, that. I was sitting in the courtyard absorbed in my music, so when he loomed over my table I mistook him for a waiter."

There was a stunned silence. Maddie's eyes grew round, but Dierdra went off into a trill of laughter. "No wonder he came home like a wounded bear."

Leighton looked at Maddie. After her initial shock,

she seemed on the point of some emotion, and he did not want it to be anger again.

"I asked him to get me another brandy and water."

Maddie clapped her hand over her mouth and squeaked, sending Dierdra into renewed bouts of mirth. They had to stop for Dierdra to catch her breath.

"Well, it was not funny at the time. He was ready to take my head off. I am surprised he didn't call me out."

Maddie gasped. "Don't tell me. You went into your studious act and he decided you were harmless."

"Yes, and he did not forbid the lessons."

"I know," Dierdra said. "But that was because he wanted to and that made Mother in favor of them."

"I would have thought they would both agree I am not suitable company for you."

"No, they never agree on anything," Dierdra said. "As Maddie pointed out, I can use that to my advantage."

Leighton blinked. "I am sure you can. Shall we go, ladies? I will not make much of an impression if I'm late."

Maddie made sure she was back in the drawing room twenty minutes before the lesson was to begin, but so was Dierdra. There was no opportunity for private speech with Leighton. In fact, the whole family was present for the start of the lesson. Leighton must have thought to drive them away with a series of scales.

"But I want to play something real," Dierdra insisted.

"Very well." He riffled through the pile of music on the piano. "Here's a piece that would suit you. A Beethoven sonata."

"I have started learning that one already."

After listening to the first dozen bars, Leighton

stilled her hands gently and said, "This is a very delicate piece, well suited to your touch. But try to play the beginning as you would stroke a tiny kitten or a little bird. Think of the piano as something alive and yet you must keep the tempo. Go head, try again."

There was such a marked improvement in her performance that Maddie felt herself staring in wonder. It was as though the piano was speaking, an illusion she frequently had when Leighton was playing. Dierdra stopped and let out a sigh. "That is as far as I have practiced."

"Do you hear the difference?"

"Most certainly."

At some point Lady Haddon must have left, but Sir Phillip stayed for the whole lesson and nodded with approval when Mrs. Marsden told Leighton to come again the day after tomorrow.

"Tomorrow we go on a picnic into the country," Dierdra confided. "Father, may Mr. Stone come? I shall ride my new mare."

"Mr. Stone is certainly welcome to ride along, if he desires and he has a horse."

Maddie thought the man was using that to stop Leighton, picturing a poor music master scouring Bath for a mount.

"What about you, Maddie?" Leighton asked. "Do you ride tomorrow?"

"No, I shall go in the carriage."

"You can ride Jasper," he offered. "You have before, and he likes you."

"Jasper is here? But I-I have no saddle."

"Oh, I can take care of that," Leighton insisted.

"But I brought no riding habit." She flushed and sent

him a speaking look.

Dierdra turned to her. "I have three. You can wear one of mine. It will be so much more fun this way."

There was no other objection Maddie could think to raise. Besides, she loved to ride and had a particular fondness for old Jasper. But she hated admitting her poverty. She had not brought a riding dress because she had none. Indeed, all the finery she now wore and the pin money in her pocket were provided by Patience.

Dierdra smiled. "That's all settled. See you tomorrow at ten, Mr. Stone."

He half expected Sir Phillip to raise some other impediment, but the look on his face was one of fondness. So the man really loved his daughter. That meant her case was not hopeless. He might not force her into a loveless marriage, as he was sure Maddie's mother had been forced, perhaps such a match as his parents had suffered.

If only Maddie would make up with him, he would guard his tongue and try not to anger her again. Finally, everyone else left and Maddie ignored him while tidying up the music.

"I think I need to apologize again."

"For what? You haven't done anything lately."

He came to stand behind her and wrap his arms around her. "For ever thinking that what I did in Spain was important, for letting it, or the bridge, or anything else be more important to me than you."

She froze in his arms. "But your work did matter. Even I realize that."

"It did not matter as much as the work you were doing at Longbridge."

She turned in his arms. "I was happy to do that. It is

what you intended, isn't it? That's why you sent me the money."

"I had hoped you would spend some on it on yourself."

"When there was such need all around me? It wasn't as though your mother would notice, and in those days, Ross and Amy could not afford to take care of any but their own people. Of course, I had to secret the money from Father, not spend too much at once, so he would not notice."

"I know that now. I should always have known you would sacrifice your own happiness for the least of my people. But I should not have let you. I counted on you more than I had any right to."

Maddie looked up at him, a faint smile trembling on those strawberry lips of hers. "Just promise me one thing."

"Only one? What is it?"

"That you will stop hiding things from me. If we are to be married, we must share everything, the good and the bad, the joys and the risks as well."

"I will tell you everything," he vowed.

She let him kiss her then, and her scent, faintly of oranges like the bush in the yard at the vicarage, reminded him of her innocence. He must never do anything to hurt her again.

Chapter Fourteen

The next morning Leighton found that Prad's Hotel did not have a sidesaddle after all. But he had inquired early, so he had time to buy one. Maddie would need one anyway, and it could be one of his wedding presents to her.

Before he left the hotel, he was joined by Dr. Murray and Lieutenant Reid, both mounted. Reid had lengthened his left stirrup to accommodate his stiff leg. At the appointed hour, they trotted up Richmond Hill with Leighton mounted on Chandros and leading Jasper. Sir Phillip was in the stable yard of Marsden House supervising the saddling of the horses.

"Where did you get that gray colt?" he asked Leighton.

"He comes from Spain of the Andalusian stock. I plan to use him as a stud."

"Fine-looking animal."

Leighton dismounted to give him a chance for a closer inspection.

The back door of the house opened and Maddie came out first, dressed in an emerald-green habit and a forage cap adorned with iridescent feathers. Leighton stared, for it was the perfect color to set off her eyes. He would have to remember that. He also reminded himself not to say anything stupid today.

"Well, come, come, ladies," Sir Phillip said. "Or it

will be mid-afternoon before we find a place to spread your picnic lunch."

Because he was holding Jasper's reins, Leighton got to help Maddie mount. He also rode beside her to make sure Jasper behaved for her. The plan was to ride up Chippenham Road, then along farm lanes, making a loop around the hill that overlooked Charmey Down. The carriage with the older ladies and the gig carrying the footmen and *al fresco* luncheon restricted them to roads rather than a cross-country romp. Leighton found himself glad, since it would give him more time to talk to Maddie.

Reid started out next to Dierdra, but Gifford, after talking to Sir Phillip for a while, dropped back and angled Reid out of the way. He started pointing out to Dierdra houses along the way and even cows and sheep. Leighton thought she tolerated him remarkably well.

"You look lovely today, Maddie."

"Thank you. I have been trying to think how long it's been since I've ridden."

"Six years." Leighton finally looked back over those years and realized something. They had been exciting ones for him, dangerous even. But for Maddie, with nothing to look forward to at the end, it must have been drudgery. He had accused her father of turning her into a servant, but he had been guilty of far worse. "That too is my fault."

"But at least now I know why. You trusted me with your tenants, though I think you might have told me what you were doing even if I couldn't help. Especially since you told Ross."

He turned to her and found her eyes no longer contained condemnation, just understanding. "You are right. I should have told you. It was just that I didn't want to promise anything, in case…"

She shook her head and smiled. "Leighton, even a broken promise is better than no promise at all."

"I had not thought of it that way. Do you forgive me, yet again?"

"Yes, but do not make a habit of concealing things from me."

"I promise you will know my mind in all matters from this day forward." Chandros tossed his head a little, fighting the bit.

"He wants to run," Maddie said. "At this snail's pace we will be past dark getting home."

"We cannot run off from the rest of them."

"Just as we cannot elope. We finally understand each other. We must make our families understand us."

"You don't ask much, but I will see what I—I mean, I will consult you about it when the time comes."

They had come along a road that skirted the base of the hill, climbing as it went. Leighton wondered if they would find themselves trapped on the top, but so many cart tracks crossed it that he felt sure they would find one to carry them down again.

They heard Gifford start an argument with Dierdra, and finally she spurred her horse ahead of the party.

Sir Phillip made no remark but to warn Gifford he would have to learn to mind his tongue.

"Poor Dierdra," Leighton said. "I had thought her a spoiled beauty, but I see now how sorely her patience is tried. We must see what we can do to help her."

Maddie filled Leighton in on how she had been coaching Dierdra to stand her ground against Gifford. He laughed at her ingenuity. After another few minutes she grew silent.

"That's odd," Maddie said. "We have not caught up with Dierdra, and we should have by now. I can see half a mile ahead, and she is not there on the road."

"She must have taken a wrong turn. That sheep track, the one that branched off back there. She must have taken that by mistake."

"Oh, Leighton, please go after her. She is not an experienced rider. Who knows what could happen?"

"Right." He turned Chandros and cantered back, spinning the horse to take the lower trail.

"Where is Leighton going?" Reid asked.

"We fear Dierdra may have taken a wrong turn and he is going to check. I think I shall go too."

"Where is everyone going?" Sir Phillip demanded after Reid followed Maddie.

"To look for Dierdra," Murray said as he too turned his horse.

When Maddie caught sight of Dierdra's red habit, the blood froze in her veins. The girl was struggling with the mare and mistakenly backing it off the edge of a hill.

"My God," Reid said under his breath. He began riding faster, as did Maddie. Then she saw Leighton appear from under the brow of the hill, galloping Chandros deliberately toward the edge. He grabbed Dierdra off her mare with his right arm just as her horse staggered backward and fell over the hill. Dierdra's weight pulled Leighton off his horse—as he must have planned, for Chandros went over the edge as well.

When Maddie rode up, she saw Leighton clinging to a handful of gorse, with Dierdra's dead weight in his other arm while he scrabbled for a foothold with his boots.

"Don't move!" Reid shouted as he halted his horse and did a running dismount that must have hurt. He drew a knife from somewhere and slashed one rein off his bridle. He tossed an end to Dierdra, but she was too faint to grab hold.

Murray dismounted and ran to add his weight to the end of the rein. Maddie managed to get down on her own and ran to the group. "Dierdra, you must stop crying and take hold of the rein. Please, we will have you up in a trice if you can only think clearly for a minute."

"My mare! I have killed her."

"Perhaps not," Leighton said with a grunt.

Finally Dierdra grasped the rein with one hand and let go of Leighton's neck. By then her father was there, and Gifford, who had caused it all. When they pulled Dierdra up, she collapsed into her father's arms, crying. Gifford started chewing at her immediately, leaving just Murray, Reid, and Maddie to pull Leighton to safety.

"Gifford, shut up about the mare," Sir Phillip said. "Can't you see she feels badly enough? It could be her lying down there."

"I've killed her," Dierdra moaned.

Leighton walked to the edge again to peek over.

"Leighton, are you trying to give us heart failure again?" Maddie demanded.

"Well, Chandros slid down all right. He may have a skinned a heel, mind you, but he's standing. I'm going down."

"What about the mare?" Gifford demanded.

"She's on her back, lodged against a tree. She may be alive but too terrified to move. I'm going down."

"How?" Reid asked.

"This trail must lead down after switching back.

Who can lend me a horse?"

"Take mine," Sir Phillip said. "I intend to turn the expedition around. I don't think any of us are in the mood for a picnic after this."

"Sorry, Maddie," Leighton said as he mounted.

"Just don't get yourself killed."

"I'll be careful. I promise."

As they rode on to find the switchback, Leighton recalled that Maddie had given him that warning with resignation rather than anger. That was a relief.

"What do you think?" Reid asked as they dismounted near Chandros a few minutes later.

A cursory glance proved what Leighton had suspected. He had a scrape on his rear hock but was not even lame.

"I never thought I would need my pistol on a picnic," Reid said as the mare lunged, then grew still.

"I don't think we need it now, but if you have that knife, it would be useful."

Reid pulled out a boot dirk and handed it to him. Leighton cut the mare's cinch, freeing the animal but not helping her upside-down condition.

"We need to turn her."

"You'll get yourself kicked in the head," Reid warned.

"Are you willing to grab the front feet?"

"Oh, why not? It's been a perfectly disastrous day up until now."

Leighton spoke soothing words to the mare and got hold of the uphill hind leg, dodging the other. Reid did the same with the front and at a word they rolled the horse downhill. The small tree against which she was lodged cracked and fell, leaving a short stump. She now rested in the V on her belly on top of the loose saddle.

"Well, she's still stuck," Reid said.

"But more able to consider her situation. Let her rest for a moment. No, I'll bring Chandros over to her. She was interested in him before. Possibly that is why she was so high strung. I swear, a mare in heat is a more dangerous ride than a stud any day."

Leighton led the colt toward the mare. The two touched noses and nickered to each other in that high-pitched squeal denoting sexual interest. Then Reid held Chandros while Leighton bent one of the mare's hind legs up and got the ankle over the tree trunk. The mare was still blowing and heaving. Before she could realize what he was doing, Leighton doubled the other hind leg up as though he was going to give her a boost.

She gave a tentative shove, pushing off against Leighton's thigh and knocking him over, but she was free. Of course then she expected to pursue the romance, but Leighton came around to take the colt's bridle and managed to quiet him while Reid examined the mare.

"How badly is she hurt?"

"You're not going to believe this, but other that this scrape above her eye she doesn't seem to have taken any harm."

"That's a surprise and a relief."

"I was not looking forward to reporting to Miss Haddon that we had to shoot the creature."

"Nor I." Leighton chuckled. "Too bad it wasn't Gifford who rolled down the hill. I would not hesitate to put a bullet between his eyes if he broke something."

Reid laughed. "Well, that would assure your position in the household. I think Sir Phillip has concluded Gifford is a dunderhead."

"My position? What, as music master?"

"No, as a suitor for Dierdra," Reid said, then led the mare toward his horse, removing one of her reins to repair his damaged bridle.

Leighton realized Reid had ridden down the hill with only one rein. His horse must be very well trained. "I have no such intent." He loaded the mare's saddle onto Chandros and tied it in place. He wanted to observe his horse's gait more before he surrendered Sir Haddon's horse. Chandros had saved the day, and he would not ride him lame.

"What then is your reason for inflicting yourself on the Haddons?"

"Inflicting?" He laughed again and told Reid the truth. "Maddie, of course."

Leighton thought the lieutenant looked skeptical. Then Reid smiled at him, though surely he must be in pain from the day's work. Leighton knew *he* was. He would have a fine set of bruises on his side and thigh, but what he mostly felt was fatigue. He'd been used to getting extra sleep to finish repairing his lungs. In the excitement of saving Dierdra, he had forgotten that feeling of absolute exhaustion that came over him when he wasn't yet fully recovered.

They were greeted as heroes when they brought all back up the hill. Dierdra looked on Leighton as though he was some victorious knight. He gave credit to Reid's quick thinking and told Dierdra to thank him for her horse's life. That brought a puzzled expression to Reid's face.

By the time they had ridden back to Marsden House, Leighton's right side was throbbing in good earnest from landing on his ribs and shoulder after grabbing Dierdra from her toppling horse. He was now used to clearing his lungs with a brandy and water, then throwing himself down for a nap when he was tired, but there had been no chance today. In fact, he had not eaten since dinner the night before, and he once or twice nodded off on the way back to Bath. Lieutenant Reid had to call his name to bring him around.

As they dismounted in the stable yard at Marsden House, Leighton stumbled against his mount and Reid steadied him. Maddie was there in an instant. She must have been watching him on the return trip. To his surprise, Sir Phillip came to help him.

"I am amazed. Not only did you save my daughter, but the two of you salvaged a horse I had given up for dead."

"I'm just glad Dierdra wasn't hurt," Leighton said as he leaned against Chandros. "Let us hope this will not give her a fear of riding."

"Never mind that for now. Come inside for some brandy. You look done in."

Leighton swayed slightly. "As appealing as that sounds, I think I had best get to the hotel before I fall asleep on my feet."

He felt himself stumble again, and Maddie came to hold him up. He gave a grunt of pain when she brushed his side.

"What is it, Leighton? Not just your lungs."

"Bruised ribs is all."

"Then you must come in until you are tended to," Sir Phillip said. "Dr. Murray can take care of you. It is the least we can do."

"Dark," Leighton said. It was getting dark—or was it just his vision going furry around the edges? Sure enough, the world started disappearing until all he could see was straight in front of his eyes—Maddie's concerned face. He wanted to tell her not to worry. He had passed out before and knew he would be fine, but he was so tired…

"He's going down," Reid said, as though Leighton was a horse and could not understand him.

"But all I need…"

****

Not being able to breathe was not a new experience but was always startling when it woke you up. Leighton fought the covers until he could heave himself up onto his elbow and cough. Someone was trying to drown him with a glass of water, and he was surprised again to discover it was Maddie.

"What the devil?" he gasped. "Where am I?"

"Marsden Hall. Don't you remember? You fainted in the courtyard."

"More like I fell asleep on my feet. What are you doing here alone with me?" Except for his small-clothes, he had been stripped and was lying in a strange bed with his chest and arms exposed. He was alone with Maddie, just as he had wanted. If only his ribs did not feel like they were on fire, it would be an amorous situation. And the look in Maddie's eyes, though admiring, probably had nothing to do with his physique.

"I convinced Mrs. Marsden that we are such old childhood friends there could be no impediment to my nursing you, that in fact it would be expected of me. Dr. Murray is still tending to Dierdra."

Leighton was leaning on his left elbow, regarding her smug assurance. Then he suddenly recalled the entire day. "Good Lord, what happened to my horses?"

Maddie gave an exasperated sigh. "You almost get yourself killed saving Dierdra, and all you can think of are your horses? We left them dripping sweat in the courtyard and now they have both taken a chill and died. What do you think happened to them? The grooms are cooling them under Reid's supervision."

"Sorry, I am not thinking clearly. I have to get word to Tibbs."

"Who is Tibbs?" Maddie asked as she adjusted his pillows and pulled the covers up over him.

The brush of her hand across his naked flesh caused him a quick intake of breath. There were some sensations that took precedence over pain. Beyond the aching need she awoke in him was a satisfaction that she cared so much about him.

"My man. Could you get a servant to go to him at Prad's Hotel? Tell him I need the tea mixture Cook gave me. It will take care of this cough."

"Very well. Perhaps I'd best send for some of your clothes, too." She sat at the small desk against the inner wall to pen a note as Leighton watched her with satisfaction. She had thrown off her jacket but still wore the white shirt and jabot from this morning. She had tucked the tail of the riding habit up into her waistband, revealing a glimpse of lace petticoat. Soon she would have no secrets from him, so he wanted to make sure there was nothing either physical or mental that he was withholding. Still, his brain was a little too fogged right now for any more confessions.

She must have realized he was watching her. She turned to look at him and tried to smile but had to close her eyes when the tears came. "You were shot in Spain," she said with a watery laugh.

"It was nothing. And it happened years ago. Nothing to cry over now."

She came and bent over him, took his face between her hands and deliberately kissed him, trailing her now-loose tresses over his naked arms. After a long minute, he groaned and laid his head back on the pillow.

"If this is how you treat a wounded man, it is small inducement to keep myself safe."

"Ah, but you do not know what I will do for you if you manage to come home whole. Something to think about for the future."

"The prospect of coming home to you is not so far away. Thank you, Maddie." Leighton closed his eyes, willing the cough to go away. But the very act of lying down seemed to bring it on, so he raised his head and stared at the fireplace.

"I swear to you it is not smoking," she replied as she went to the desk and picked up her note.

"Just checking."

The door opened and Mrs. Marsden carried a tray in. "Here we have something for that cough."

Leighton saw Maddie wrinkle her nose at the bowl, but at this point he was willing to try anything.

"What is your secret potion?" he croaked.

"Beef broth. Drink it up."

"I'll just send for your things then," Maddie said and exited.

The broth did put some life into him and even stilled the cough momentarily. Dr. Murray came in with Sir Phillip. Leighton sucked in an unsteady breath when a cold hand examined his bruised side.

"One rib is cracked," Murray said, "and you will wear those bruises for a while. You should have said you were hurt before we let you ride the whole way back."

"I don't think it's serious."

Sir Phillip loomed over the bed. "I think we should listen to Dr. Murray on this."

"Hmm, well, by itself, no, it's not a serious injury, but you also have bruises on your shoulder and thigh, a lump on the back of your head, and your original inflammation in the lungs. Taken altogether, I recommend a few days in bed."

"A few days?" Leighton complained, then subsided, for if they were going to let Maddie nurse him, it might be just the ticket to get all the time he could wish to talk to her.

"And no riding," Murray added.

"But my horses—"

"Will be fine in my stable. Stone, you just saved my daughter's life. At least consent to be my house guest until I am confident you are not going to keel over from the aftereffects."

"Well, I did come to Bath to rest. I don't suppose it matters where I do it."

Content with Leighton's capitulation, Sir Phillip retreated to the desk. The doctor made a more minute examination of the rest of his scratches and bruises, spent what Leighton considered an inordinate amount of time taping the ribs, then sat down to write out some instructions. Leighton was arguing against laudanum and saying brandy would help, when the door opened to admit Tibbs and Maddie. Leighton was beginning to think the room a little crowded.

"My lord, what happened?"

His retainer looked concerned, and he had let slip his title. Damn. "It is nothing, Tibbs, a slight fall off my horse."

"Is aught broken?"

"Just a rib. Did you bring the tea?"

"Right here, sir. I shall go to the kitchen and make it up myself." With that he hastened out, and Maddie ducked out with him. Had that really been worry that had sat on Tibbs's brow? Did the fellow actually care what happened to him?

"What did he call you?" Sir Phillip asked.

"No telling. Poor fellow. Tibbs is from the stews of London. Anyone who doesn't drop his H's is like a king to him."

Dr. Murray threw Leighton a penetrating look.

Sir Phillip folded his arms. "Just who are you, Stone? A music master who rides like a demon and tosses his life away as though it is nothing? You are not the average Oxford-educated son of a clergyman."

"No, it is Maddie whose father is a clergyman. Mine was…a farmer."

Dr. Murray blew out a slow breath. "You may as well tell him, Stone. I have seen that look, and he will find out anyway."

"Well, I do not suppose it matters, though all I wanted was a quiet trip to Bath. My father was Longbridge."

Sir Phillip stared at him "The Earl of Longbridge?"

Leighton nodded and Sir Phillip slowly began to laugh. "And here I was warning you away from my daughter."

"As well you should. Dierdra is far too young and impressionable to be thinking on anything but parties and dresses."

"And your connection to Miss Westlake?"

"I came looking for her when she disappeared from my estate. I was relieved to find her with her sister rather than murdered somewhere."

"So how do you two know each other?"

"Dr. Murray treated me before."

"At Longbridge?"

"Ah, no," Murray said. "It was in Portugal. Got himself shot between the ribs by a French sniper."

"Portugal. That explains the scar, but what were you doing in Portugal?"

"Well, I had heard it was splendid country. Thought I might have a look round."

Murray chuckled. "Being as Sir Phillip is in the House of Commons and on the naval appropriations committee, I think it might be safe to tell him."

"The war is over," Leighton said.

"Tell me what?"

"Stone here assisted Captain Scoville in his work for Lord Wellington, with the French dispatches and writing our own codes—"

"Oh, my God!" Sir Phillip said slowly as he brought his hand to his brow. "You are *that* music master, the one who played at the parties and then spent the night deciphering."

"You've heard of me? But how?"

"As you say, the war is over and men seem to feel they can speak freely now."

"Then letting my mother spend two weeks in London was not a safe idea. If she had any intelligence at all, she might have discovered what I have been doing these past six years."

"Well, well." Sir Phillip got up to leave, a pleased smile on his face.

"Does this mean you are going to blab this all over Bath?"

"I might tell my wife."

Leighton rolled his gaze heavenward.

"If I did, there would be no impediment to your courting Dierdra."

"I can think of one. I do not love her."

"Well, she is certainly in love with you."

He went out then, and Leighton leaned back on the nest of pillows.

"Now, why would she fall in love with me?"

"You who saved her from certain death and brought her mare home with hardly a scratch? I cannot imagine." Murray hummed to himself as he mixed a decoction and left it on the nightstand.

How could things have gotten so out of hand in one day? At least Maddie was not angry with him over rescuing Dierdra. In fact, she was the one who had asked him to go after her. He would have to mention that, if her anger followed on the heels of her concern as it often did. But if anyone deserved the credit for saving Dierdra, it was Maddie for noticing she was missing. He would have to save that argument in case Dierdra appeared too interested.

For now, he needed sleep if he was to survive Maddie's nursing. The pull of need, desire, and downright hunger that had started that day in the lane was now a constant gnawing. When they were separated, his feelings had leaned toward worry, but now with her so close and touching him so intimately, it felt almost as though they were married, as though his goal loomed within reach.

He was desperately afraid he was going to do

something passionately improper, and that Maddie in her present state of mind might let him. He was hunting about in his mind for something to distract both of them, and he thought of the code, but his mind was too fuzzy to focus on it.

There came a moment when everything stopped aching and he lay very still, thinking of how he would make a fountain and lily pond in the courtyard. The flagstone area between the ancient sprawl of house and the stable had always seemed cold and untidy with weeds. He could have some of the stones pulled up to repair the broken ones and create a garden area outside the back door of the house. He drew the plans in his mind. In the morning he would tell Maddie about them, and they would work on them together. That would be more fun than worrying over that stupid piece of music.

Chapter Fifteen

Maddie was preparing another poultice for Leighton's ribs while Tibbs steeped his tea. Acting as Leighton's nurse gave Maddie even more status in the household. In the kitchen the entire staff, including now Tibbs, bowed to her every command.

After learning of Leighton's title, Lady Haddon voiced no objection to Maddie nursing him. Probably she thought there could never be a relationship between Maddie and Leighton other than servant and master. Maddie could not blame Dierdra for worshiping Leighton. He was a hero. And that was something Maddie was going to have to accept about him, that he might throw his life away to save another's, even when he barely knew the person. That was the way Leighton was.

For now all she could do was be there to pick up the pieces. But when they were married, she would see to it that he did not come in the way of dangerous temptations. She realized she really believed now that they would be married, that nothing could bar their way. On her own she would have seen only the impediments, the dark patches. Leighton made her see the possibilities. They were a good pairing, a pessimist and an optimist. Perhaps, over time, they would change each other and not argue so very much.

Maddie realized she was taking on a lifetime of

worry as Leighton's wife. But she would still worry about him even if they were not married. And as his wife, she might exercise an element of control and prevent such accidents.

As Tibbs loaded the teapot onto the tray, she amended that. Leighton was also a mathematician and could calculate without thinking if something was a lost cause. So he would do his utmost, but he would know how risky something was and would not precisely throw his life away. That was a point in his favor. She folded the poultice and nodded to Tibbs. He picked up the tray, which now contained a substantial meal besides the medicine and tea.

Yes, Leighton needed her. She tapped on his door and opened it when he said, "Come."

He pushed together sheets of music and other notes in preparation to finally getting *a decent meal*. She took the stacks of papers away and put them on the desk. He would tell her what they were about in good time. Until this past six years, they had shared every confidence. So she had not missed him just physically but as a friend. She had him back now and would not let anyone or anything come between them again.

Leighton allowed them to replace the poultice before he ate because it did feel good against his ribs. Of course it was more fun being tended by Maddie without his man present. And he was getting a little sick of Tibbs's bowing and scraping. As soon as he was able, he would have to do something to infuriate the man and get back on a more normal footing.

Maddie was another matter. She sat patiently in a chair by the window while he ate, a large apron over her old brown dress. She worked at some sewing while Tibbs fussed with his clothes. Leighton ate quickly both because he was hungry and because he had something to discuss with Maddie, several things.

The doctor calling up his memories of the war had put him in mind again of the codes he had solved. And no matter how he had tried to banish the scrap of music from his mind, he had worked on it in his sleep. It had to be a coded message. Why else would someone search his rooms? Fortunately he had put that bit in his wallet, so they had not found it. But why had it been sent to him? Figuring that out was more important than mapping a garden at Longbridge—more immediate, at any rate.

"Oh," Tibbs said. "I near forgot. A letter came for you."

"Another letter? I hope it's something I can read."

He took the folded sealed paper from Tibbs. "Oh, it's from Ross." When he broke the seal, there was a smaller note inside for Maddie. "From my sister Amy, I take it. She probably wants to wish us happy."

Tibbs arched an eyebrow at the revelation, then bestowed the smaller note on a surprised Maddie before he exited with a bundle of laundry.

"How do they know we are here? Oh, you wrote to Ross."

"Yes, in case anything went amiss, I wanted Ross to know where I was." The letter contained only farm news and bits about the children. "It looks as if the crops have not washed out. That's a bit of luck."

When Leighton looked at Maddie's tragic face he knew something was wrong. "What is it? Is someone ill?"

"No," she said coldly. "Your tenants all go on well. Is it true that you swam the river during the flood?"

Leighton knew he had to answer carefully. "I don't know that I would call it swimming. I got the rope to the other side so we could start the bridge."

"You could have drowned."

"Well, no. I had a rope tied about me. If I hadn't reached the other side they would have pulled me back."

"This is why you are ill. Was there ever anything so stupid? You could have waited until the water went down."

"Yes and perhaps have the carriage with Susan, Amy, Ross, and Mother swept downstream instead, when they tried to ford somewhere else."

"Ross would never have been so stupid. Why are you?"

"It's my job."

"To be stupid?"

"To do what has to be done." Leighton sat up and let the sheets fall away. "Listen to me, Maddie."

"Go on being stupid. Get up and pass out on us."

"Maddie, the river bends there. I could see the current would carry me to the other shore."

"So you calculated the risk and took your life in your hands again."

"It was not something I could ask anyone else to do." He could see emotions at war in her face. Regret, anger, and finally resignation. "Maddie, what are you thinking?"

"That there isn't a lot of difference between being a hero and being an idiot."

"A hero? For what?"

"For doing what no one else would do." She stood and came to him. "Is it odd that I should be both angry and proud of you at the same time?" Her arms snaked around his neck and she rested them on his shoulders.

"I don't know," he said. "I've never been in love before."

He captured her waist in his hands, which fit almost the whole way around it. "I have often wondered how someone as delicate as you can do all the visits, nurse all the sick and carry food to them, and probably do it all without your father's knowledge or consent."

"It is *my* job. Perhaps it's not as spectacular as the insane tasks you set for yourself."

He leaned slowly forward and kissed her, his head swimming with the giddiness of the moment. She let him take a breath and he said, "But yours are the more necessary tasks. As you said, my stupidity could have waited. It was only—"

"Only what?"

"After being driven away by your father, I felt so defeated I had to do something."

"Coming for me would have been more to the point."

"I know that now. I swear that is the last time I will put duty before your welfare."

Maddie laughed and kissed him again.

"What's the matter? Don't you believe me?"

"I believe you mean it when you say it. At least I will be with you from now on to moderate your insanity."

"So you are not angry with me this time?"

"Yes, of course I am, but I am not letting that get in the way anymore."

"Does Amy say anything useful in your letter that does not upset the apple cart?"

"Only how much you are loved by your people and how angry your mother is."

"I don't suppose she had the chimneys cleaned."

"No, new hangings for her bedroom."

"Well, that's harmless enough." He pressed his mouth to her ripe lips again and felt another delightful spin of dizziness. When she finally drew back to look at him, he said, "Much as I would like to go on kissing you all day, there is something to discuss where we can work together."

"Something to do with Longbridge?"

"Not yet. Maddie, could you hand me that stack of papers again?"

She looked at him as though humoring an invalid. "I think you should rest now, instead."

He waited while she arranged his pillows and drew up the covers as though she was his wife taking care of him after an accident. She made him forget the urgency of everything except being with her. Perhaps the code could wait until Maddie was done torturing him. He must be getting better, for he scarcely thought about his injuries when she was in the room.

He wanted so much to project them into that happy future where Maddie was safely his and nothing could come between them. He took it as a matter of course that he would from time to time come to grief with a horse and be laid up. That was part of his job. He hoped that caring for him would be part of hers.

"Why are you staring at me like that?" Maddie asked.

"Merely admiring how well you do this."

"Do what?"

"Take care of people."

"I have had more than enough practice. And they are your tenants. Taking care of you puts me in mind of something I have been meaning to ask you."

"I am afraid to know what that is."

"I am happy that you were able to rescue Dierdra, but did you have to leap off a cliff to do it?" Her voice rose near the end, not in anger but fear.

"I am sorry, Maddie, if I worried you, but I had to get her off that horse. If she had hung on when that mare tumbled down the hill, she would have been pinned underneath her and died a painful death."

Maddie sighed. "I know that. Too bad she couldn't jump off."

"You know how hard it is to extricate yourself from a sidesaddle."

"I would have managed it."

"I know I could have relied on you leaping off yourself, but you would not have backed a horse over a hill to begin with."

Her gaze took on a more martial glare. "I see, so you would risk your life for Dierdra but not for me? I'm just not the sort of girl who needs a desperate rescue."

"You would never have done anything so crack-brained to begin with." He had boosted himself up again and was regarding her from a sitting position, unable to argue lying down. "You shouldn't be jealous of Dierdra because you are more capable than she is."

Maddie stared at him in puzzlement. "You didn't answer my question. Did you have to ride your horse straight at the cliff?"

He could see now it was worry and not jealousy that motivated her. "It wasn't a cliff, just a very steep hill. I had to aim for the right side of her horse to make sure I could snatch her off the sidesaddle easily. She would have hung up on the horns if I had tried to get her off the other side. Any more questions? For I have something important to discuss with you."

Maddie paced the small room. "I see. You calculated just how to save her and were in no danger at all."

"You are making my head spin. Come here and sit down." Once she was on the bed, Leighton took her hand and tried to compose something reassuring to say without lying to her. "I promise I will never go to war again, I will not swim any more swollen rivers, and I will not go riding with any young ladies likely to need rescuing. But if I see you in danger, or one of our children, don't expect me to value my own skin."

"Our children?"

"I think we would make good parents."

Maddie nodded, her green eyes merry. "Yes, my constancy coupled with your idiocy. They should come out quite normal by the standards of the day."

Leighton burst into laughter and started to cough.

"What did you want to discuss?"

"That pile of paper I have been working at. Do you remember me saying my room had been ransacked?"

She got up and brought him the papers. "Yes, you said they had stolen your music."

He sorted through them, pushing the garden plans aside and drawing the code work onto his lap.

"But they did not get this, for I was carrying it with me. It was part of the packet I received, and the rest of that packet was taken."

He held up the paper. She scanned it, then turned it upside down. "This is the most awful piece of music I have ever seen."

"I don't think it is—music, I mean. I think it is a coded message. I have worked out several possible ways to do a simple substitution code with musical notes and symbols."

He could see she was gaping at him. Then she rested her hand on his forehead.

He laughed. "No, I am not running a fever. I am serious."

"But why, Leighton? You just said you were done with this business. Why would someone be sending you coded messages here in Bath? It makes no sense."

"I didn't think so either, unless the message was not meant for me. That would explain why my room was searched."

"But they delivered the package to your room. What did it say?"

"Mr. Stone, Prad's Hotel. Perhaps I am not the only Stone there."

"Perhaps you have rocks in your head."

"Just do me a favor and take a look at my work. See if you think it is a possibility. You said you wanted me to confide in you."

When Maddie leaned over to reach for the sheaf of papers, one lock of hair trailed along his collarbone, drawing a sigh of need from him.

She glanced skeptically at him. "I begin to think you are not as injured as we had supposed."

He grasped the lock and used it to tug her down for another kiss. "I begin to think you are not safe alone with me. How many days until your birthday?"

"Ten. Not so long to wait. It should give you time to search your conscience and make sure there is nothing else you have omitted to tell me." She took the sheaf of papers with an interested pucker between her delicate eyebrows.

"Don't let anything happen to that scrap of music. I never got it copied out."

"Very well. We will discuss this after you have slept and, I hope, come to your senses.

"That is all I ask. He lay back and decided he could sleep again with a quiet mind. Maddie had forgiven him. They were working together and had an interesting puzzle to solve. What more could he ask of life?

Chapter Sixteen

While Leighton slept, Maddie went over his notes. Though they made sense to her, none of the possible codes he had created resulted in anything but gibberish. He would be disappointed, but she thought this was a false start. He had been using the lines and spaces on the staff for positions to represent the letters *A* through *M* and the change from sharp to flat to indicate switching over to the letters *N* to *Z*. But that gave her nothing. What if she turned the idea around and made the notes the letters and their position on either a line or a space the factor that flopped from the first half of the alphabet to the second? She was busy with this when a knock came on her door and Lady Haddon stepped in.

"You promised to go with Dierdra to the lending library this afternoon."

"Yes, of course. Is she well enough?"

"I think so. I know you are devoted to Leighton, but you must not neglect the rest of us or fail to take the air yourself. You have not stepped foot outside the house since the accident."

"Sorry. I will be down as soon as I change my dress."

When the woman left, Maddie gathered up the papers. She was about to stuff them under the blotter but Leighton would laugh at that, so she pushed all of them into a pillow cover and pinned them between the lining of her old gray cloak and the outside wool. There. He would not ridicule her for that hiding place.

Dierdra could talk of nothing but Leighton and the rescue, the whole way to the library. Maddie mentioned Gifford's part in it and Dierdra decried his cowardice. That was good. Maddie pointed out Dierdra had weight now for her argument not to marry her cousin. Dierdra agreed, but this was mostly because her heart was now set on Leighton. And he was an earl. *Was there ever anything to equal it?* Maddie had to agree there was not, but she couldn't help wondering how Dierdra would feel when Leighton did not propose. She tried pointing out how vital Lieutenant Reid had been to saving her horse. Dierdra was most grateful to him but not in love with him.

The breaking of dreams was something that happened to everyone. Dierdra would have to get used to it, as she had. After all they had been through, nothing could possibly go wrong for her and Leighton now. They had only to wait for her birthday.

On her return, Maddie met Tibbs in the hall, carrying Leighton's boots newly shined and a just-pressed set of clothes. The man looked even worse than he had the afternoon before, when he'd appeared out of breath at Marsden House with the packet of tea Leighton had requested.

"Tibbs, does he mean to get up already?"

"Aye, Miss Westlake. He's had a bath and means to go down for dinner. He don't take proper care of himself. Never did. Always coming home burnt to the socket. But he hates to have anyone pay attention to his injuries, so it hasn't been easy looking after him. That cough I don't like. My sister died of the consumption, and…"

"No worries on that score. Leighton only gets this once in a while, but it takes weeks for him to get clear of it. He says he never had it the whole time he lived in London."

Tibbs averted his eyes. "No, miss, never in London."

She felt a tickle of suspicion. "What about in Spain or Portugal?" she prodded.

"Not as far as I know, nor France neither. You know about that?"

"Yes. But when was Leighton in France?"

"Not above twice, to visit someone in prison. 'E was often pitched off strange horses, but 'twas only to be expected in his line of work."

Maddie nodded, trying to assimilate everything Tibbs was telling her and wondering if it was ethical to use her wedge of familiarity to find out the extent of Leighton's activities. Of course it was. So, he still had not told her the whole truth.

"Yes, assisting Captain Scoville with the codes. Leighton told you all this?"

"Goodness no, miss. He'd never have been at liberty to do that. But my brother and I had a pint with a fella from the Ninety-First, and he told us all about Leighton."

Somehow Maddie managed to control her emotions. "I am glad the war is over, though I've no doubt I will still lose sleep over him."

"Me too, miss. Well, he means to get up. I'd best go to him."

Maddie went on to her room, intent on changing her dress to the dark green silk appropriate for a family dinner. How odd that Leighton would inspire such devotion in a servant he treated so casually. But then he had her absolute devotion, though she would be damned if she would let him know it. He was going to have to think of her for a change rather than his music, his codes, or anyone else. Still, she ran her hand up under the cloak to make sure the packet was safe before she changed for dinner.

When she went down the stairs, someone was picking out a hideous tune on the pianoforte in the drawing room. She went to see who it was.

"Leighton, has your cold affected your hearing? That is awful."

"I know. It's what I remember of that scrap of music I gave you. You have it safe?"

"Of course, and I must agree that, as music, it falls far short of the mark."

"It is not playable. Have you given any thought to its being a code?"

"I have done some work on it, but first things first. Just to clear the air, you might want to offer me some explanations for your other trips, besides to Spain."

"Other?" His eyes widened, then his face looked shot with guilt.

"France?"

She watched the full import of what she said dawn on Leighton, and his face turn sheepish. "You've been gossiping with Tibbs."

"Do you know he was worried to death over you?"

"No. I had always thought him nicely detached from my welfare, not at all likely to try to wrap me in cotton wool. I see now he is as bad as all the others."

"Be serious, Leighton. What were you doing there?"

"I had a safe conduct. I was picking up a letter from a captured officer to be sent to his family."

Maddie sighed. "No, I mean what were you *really*

doing?" She sat beside him on the piano bench.

"It was in code, of course."

He went back to picking out some notes on the pianoforte. If not for his cracked rib, she would have cuffed him.

"I knew it. You must have courted death a hundred times."

"That is all in the past. Maddie, what did that composition call to mind for you?"

She put her frustration aside to answer him. "Nothing. I have one idea I want to try, but I have not had time to work on it yet."

"Does it remind you of those puzzles Father used to set for us?"

Maddie thought back to when they had spent so much time solving Lord Longbridge's acrostics and ciphers. "I suppose, but your father has been dead for six years. Is there anyone else who would be sending you such a thing now that the war is over?"

"But it is not over, as you said. We are still at war with America. I keep wondering if this is some sort of joke."

"I would rather hope someone sent it to you by mistake, thinking you were someone else."

"Possibly. Now that I think about it, Tibbs said the man who delivered it sounded like an American. But I don't know anyone in America."

"They may know you and think you are here for some reason you know nothing about. If they did intend it for you, even by mistake, then you are not out of the war. You are in danger still."

He took his hands off the keys and smiled at her. "I don't know how much danger there is."

"Well, that is the point. You don't know. You are excited because you like danger, but I do not."

He reached toward her with his good arm and caressed her cheek. "I am sorry. You are right again. Throw the paper away, and all the decoding. We are better off out of it." He was leaning over to kiss her, but she was feeling far from loving at the moment. *Throw it away?* Was he mad? That would not make him safe.

The door to the drawing room opened, and she slid away from him as the family gathered for dinner. Dr. Murray was with them this evening. Perhaps he would scotch Leighton's intention to resume his normal activities.

"Leighton, dear boy," Lady Haddon said on their way to the dining room, "but I should call you Longbridge, though it is hard, now that we have been using your common name. I hope you are feeling better. We owe you everything for saving Dierdra."

So Haddon had told his wife he had a title. Leighton had liked her better as an enemy. "All in a day's work," he said, then pulled out her chair. "I appreciate your hospitality, but I shall be moving back to my hotel. I don't want to lose that excellent room."

Gifford grunted his approval but said nothing more under Sir Phillip's menacing stare.

In fact, except for the noise he made eating, which was considerable, Gifford was strangely silent throughout dinner. Dr. Murray carried the flag of conversation, imparting all the latest gossip in an amusing fashion.

Lady Haddon cast Gifford a look of disgust at the end of the second course of dishes and turned her smile on Leighton. "You will still play for my musical evening, won't you, Leighton?"

He swallowed and glanced toward Mrs. Marsden, wondering how it had become Lady Haddon's musicale. The older woman shrugged and smiled.

"Of course," Leighton said, "if Maddie and Dierdra will also play."

"I am not ready," Dierdra said.

"You will be," Leighton assured her. He realized he should say something just as reassuring and charming to Maddie, but he could not think what. "Maddie, will you play? You have more skill at the pianoforte than I. You just never get credit for it."

She looked surprised but smiled at him. "I shall play."

"Good, because I sent my invitations for Saturday evening," Lady Haddon said.

Leighton choked on his wine but covered it with a cough. Maddie now sent him an accusing look.

"That's only a few days from now," he finally managed to say.

Dierdra turned a worried look on him. "You said we could be ready."

"Of course we can, but we must spend every spare moment practicing."

Leighton had planned to leave after dinner, but Sir Phillip begged him to stay one more night to assure him that he had taken no serious hurt from his fall. The doctor agreed with this plan, and Leighton was almost glad he was being released. He missed his room at the hotel and that charming fountain in the courtyard. He could not really be intimate with Maddie until they were married, so there was no advantage to living under the same roof.

There was temptation, of course, though he did not

think that was intentional. She probably thought she was being sympathetic. But he didn't want Maddie's sympathy. He wanted her. And since he could not have her yet, he must busy himself with something else, or those intimate moments in his bedchamber would drive him mad.

Besides, if they were to be practicing music half the day, he would have ample opportunity to talk to her. He thought his latest capitulation would tempt Maddie into looking into the puzzle of the music with him. He loved watching the way her eyes sparkled when she was thinking. She had looked particularly dazzling in the green silk dress and he had neglected to mention it. He must get a grip.

Gifford had not come into the drawing room after dinner, and the doctor had departed. He and Maddie started discussing the selections for Saturday and he went upstairs for his portfolio of music. What he found was Tibbs organizing his room.

"Oh, no, not again!"

"It wasn't you?" the man asked as he picked up Leighton's shaving gear.

"I've been downstairs these past two hours."

"Mostly they made a mess of your music sheets. What could they have been looking for?"

"I think I know. By now they have come to the conclusion that I carry it with me. So that should prove interesting."

"I do not like the way you say 'interesting.' That usually means mending and laundering for me and more bruises and healing for you."

"Sorry I am such a trial to you."

"Then why not settle down with that nice Miss

Westlake?"

"I intend to."

Leighton took the music downstairs, knowing Maddie would chide him for mixing it up. But he would have no chance to talk to her about anything of importance until tomorrow.

Leighton went to bed wondering if it was Dr. Murray who had searched his room. But he would have had ample opportunity while Leighton was unconscious the day before. Lieutenant Reid wasn't with them tonight, but did that mean he could not have gotten into the house? Gifford, of course, was a potential suspect, but Leighton could not for the life of him imagine the man capable of intrigue.

He hoped Maddie had a clue about the solution, for he was nonplussed. He kept trying out possibilities in his mind but nothing fit neatly. Perhaps it wasn't a simple substitution cipher but a twisted path code, or a screen. Maybe even a combination. If there was a key, it could take even longer. Obviously if the message was intended for him, it did not have a key and it must have been sent by someone who knew he could solve it. Damn, but he was losing his edge. Maddie would have some ideas.

Chapter Seventeen

Leighton removed from Marsden House directly after breakfast, promising to come back at two o'clock to begin the practice sessions. He had music to pick up in town and a puzzle to solve in his head. He could picture most of the code in his mind's eye and began to wonder if he had started with a botched assumption. There were enough special symbols, including the notes themselves, for the code to be something like the Masons' cipher, but instead of cross-hatched lines and X's, the grid could be the musical staff itself.

He had lunch in the courtyard at his favorite table and put some finishing touches on Maddy's song. But his mind kept going back to the message and an odd association. He had realized before that the message was scented with pipe smoke. He had smelled that recently in Patience's morning room.

He decided on the way up the hill to call on Patience, but her butler denied her to him. He had no reason to suspect the man of lying, except for the odd notion he was being watched. He was an expert at acting normally even when he knew he was under scrutiny, but it was unnerving not to know for sure.

Arriving early at Marsden House, he went to visit his horses. Sir Phillip had insisted his head groom take care of Chandros until the scrape was on the mend. And Leighton had offered to leave Jasper there for Maddie's use. This prompted Sir Phillip to insist that Leighton stable both his mounts there for the duration of his stay in town.

It was perfect. Even after this musicale, he would have an excuse for showing up at Marsden House any time of the day or night, and if they arranged things carefully, Maddie could meet him in the garden between the house and stable.

After a short discussion with the groom, Leighton was about to go and practice on the pianoforte until Dierdra came down for her lesson. He was walking toward the house when Maddie burst out of the back door with a dossier under her arm and dark circles under her eyes.

"Where the devil have you been?" she demanded in a fierce whisper.

She was wearing a gray walking dress and had ink stains on her delicate fingers.

"Why, what's the matter? You look distressed. Come and sit in the garden." He led her through the box hedge to a remote bench not easily visible from the house.

She sat and spread the leather case open in her lap. "I have been up all night with this cipher you gave me. It is such a short message, there is little to work with."

"I know. Perhaps I was wrong and it is simply a badly written piece of music."

"No, I solved it."

"What?" He found himself staggering and got a shiver. Maddie was better at this than he was. He also felt a glow of pride in her. "God, Maddie. I wish you had been with me in Spain."

She stared raptly at him and smiled. "Thank you. It is a substitution cipher, of course, with the half note being A, the dotted half B, and so on."

"But you need four variations to get the other three fourths of the alphabet," Leighton protested.

"Didn't you notice how some notes have the staff backward and others up when they should be down?" She pointed to the scrap of paper in her lap.

"Of course!" He slapped his forehead. "Four variations."

"Yes. Staff up and to the right, the half note to the 32th note represent A to F. Staff down and right G to L, down and left M to R, and up and left for the letters left, with the last note representing X, Y and Z. So a Z would be what?"

Leighton stared into space. "A 32nd note with the staff up and left."

"Correct."

"Well, what does it say?"

"Will know location of fleet. Getting ships in train. Do you back enterprise? S-N."

"Good work, Maddie." He put his arm around her. "S-N could be Scrope-Nevins. Isn't that the name of your sister's crony?"

"True but she may not be the only S-N, or the only Scrope-Nevins on earth, and I don't think Patience knows her all that well."

"We shall have to find that out as soon as this musicale is over. Oh, God!" Leighton thought back over the last few days.

"What?"

"The last two times I called, Patience was acting nervous and kept the doors shut that lead into the adjoining salon. At first I thought she was having an affair, but—"

"A what? Patience? Are you sure that fever hasn't come back on you?"

She felt his forehead, and he loved the familiar feel of her hand on his skin. He took her hand and kissed it. "I know that was silly of me. But this could be worse. What if she is letting this Scrope-Nevins woman listen in on her guests in the hope of, of…"

"Of, what, Leighton?" Maddie snapped the folder shut and stood up to glare at him. "Spit it out. Are you accusing my sister of being a spy?"

Too late he saw the error of speculating in Maddie's presence. "Perhaps a pawn in a plot she does not understand."

"And you do? No, I will not even allow that." Maddie vaulted from the bench and brushed past him.

"Maddie, wait. That is not as bad as what I was thinking of her before."

"What, that she has a lover?" she said over her shoulder.

"No, I would not even care for that. But Patience may be no stranger to conspiracy. When your mother…took ill, you were hurried off to your sister in York, but Patience stayed home."

Maddie clutched the notes to her breast. "Yes, Patience came for me at Longbridge one evening, would not even let me say goodbye to Mother, since they thought the chance of infection so great. What of it?"

"So you never saw her. For all you know she might have been dead already."

"But she wasn't." Maddie shook her head and almost staggered. "She died the next day, and by the time word got to me I was already in York."

"They could have just had you stay with my sisters

at Longbridge."

"I never thought of that. What are you driving at?"

"That Patience was in a position to cover up for your father, if in a fit of rage he…"

"He what? Killed my mother? You are insane to suggest such a thing, such a hurtful thing."

When the tears came to her eyes, Leighton realized building a case against Patience wasn't his brightest idea, not when it distressed Maddie.

"Maddie, I am so sorry." He rushed to take her in his arms, regretting his excitement and tendency to think out loud. "I don't know what made me think of it. You are right. If I have not got a plot to work on, I make something up." He stroked her back and tried to press her head against his shoulder, but she stared at him. "You're not saying anything. What is it?"

"Sometimes I hate you, Leighton. You make me reach into the dark corners of my mind and drag out all the things I don't want to look at."

"Then you too think… I should have said nothing."

"It's only that Papa always looks at me with such contempt, and I do look like Mother—more each year, I suppose."

He could see the tears gathering in her eyes and knew he had caused this, all to prove his theory about Patience. "I'm sorry."

"It could explain why he dislikes me so, if he…"

"If he was unkind to her, that does not mean my flight of fancy is true."

"He was more than unkind to her. He never hit her, but he might as well have. She shed enough tears over his cutting remarks to fill the pond." Maddie pushed herself back from him, still clutching the case in one arm.

"Unfortunately, there is no way to prove it one way or the other," he said.

"What good would we do if we could prove it? She would still be dead." Maddie shook her head and began to back away from him.

"But you would know if you could trust him or not."

"It does not matter. I shall never go back to him."

"Then you still mean to marry me?" Leighton took a hesitant step toward her, hoping he had not again ruined his chances.

"I-I don't know. Have you got any other nasty shocks up your sleeve, or are you through making me unhappy?"

Leighton came and held her again. "I never meant to hurt you, and I will have a care never to do so again. Why do you think I moved back to my hotel when I would much rather have stayed?"

"To avoid Dierdra, of course."

"It is not fair to let her think she can have anything she wants. I hope neither of her parents have put the idea of marriage to me in her head."

"She has thought of it herself. Give her some credit. You shouldn't have let your title slip out."

"Tibbs blundered, and then Dr. Murray ratted me out, though I had asked him not to reveal my identity."

"I wonder why he told Sir Phillip."

"I cannot imagine."

"Perhaps he wants you connected to the Haddons."

"But why?"

"Or wants you to stay here. That gives him more of an entrée."

"He knew them before I did. I imagine he could call here any time he pleased."

"But not have the run of the house."

Leighton stiffened, and Maddie glanced up at him. "What is it?"

"Last night the music in my room was all mixed up. And someone had gone through the rest of my things."

"Could it have been the doctor looking for this?"

"Do you feel unsafe having that?"

"No, but I don't want anyone clubbing you over the head for it. If this was meant for the doctor—and he does have the room next to your suite at the hotel—then we have to assume he does not know Mrs. Scrope-Nevins is his contact, but he must know who sent it."

"And he is to supply the location of the British Fleet to…whom? The Americans? Certainly they can't mean to attack us here. It sounds as though the peace negotiations have begun."

"Who else would want to know where the fleet is?" Maddie speculated.

"The French, if they were planning anything. But they've surrendered. Napoleon has been shipped off to Elba with an honor guard of a thousand troops. Too good a treatment for him, if you ask me."

"But what is to prevent his men from overpowering his guard and leaving?"

"It is an island," Leighton reminded her.

"Which could be why they want to know where the fleet is."

Leighton froze and looked at her. "You are giving me cold chills."

"When they say *back the enterprise*, they must mean are you going to supply the money."

"There are enough idle vessels in Bristol to transport a thousand men. Though the captains might not be willing once they knew their destination. But once docked at Elba…"

"Now, where would they go," she asked. "Mexico? France has interests there."

"Not Napoleon. He would go back to France. It seems preposterous, and yet…"

"How can we find out?"

Leighton inclined his head. "By asking Patience if she sent the packet. She never could lie worth a damn. If she is lying, we will know."

Maddie swallowed and took a deep breath. "When?"

"Tomorrow, and not in the Pump Room. In her drawing room. I plan to invite us to tea there."

The back door was flung open and Dierdra appeared. Leighton and Maddie leaped apart as though they had been doing something wrong.

"There you are. I have been practicing my piece. Do you want to hear it?"

"Of course," Leighton said. "We are just coming."

Leighton pronounced Dierdra's piano solo nearly ready except for one or two parts that he demonstrated for her. He laid out the program for the whole evening, an ambitious enterprise for just the three of them, but the songs should not give the girls much trouble. The guests at Lady Haddon's musicale were unlikely to be interested in anything but the refreshments.

He switched their rehearsal time to morning on the morrow. When he got back to the hotel, he sent a note round to Maddie's sister, asking if they might call. Then he asked Raymond, the footman, to find out if there were any other Stones registered at the hotel.

He had been so busy he had forgotten his aching ribs and need for sleep. His goal, to expose Patience Carter, was not a noble one, and he sincerely hoped he was wrong in suspecting her, on all points.

To his surprise, he received a note before dinner that she expected him and Maddie for tea. It bothered him that she'd played into their hands. In his experience, that meant she was planning something he had not even taken into account. He scrutinized her handwriting, but it was nothing like the block printing on the now-missing envelope.

The doctor ran into him in the lobby and asked if he could join him for dinner. Leighton agreed.

"I have not seen Lieutenant Reid lately," he said as they took seats in the hotel dining room.

"He had to leave town on an errand."

Leighton nodded, desperately wanting to satisfy his curiosity, but if he suspected the doctor, then the reverse might be true. It did not pay to be inquisitive unless you already knew the answers to the questions you were going to pose.

"This musicale will be quite an event," the doctor said. "The salons should be full."

"Full?"

"Yes, Lady Haddon has invited half of Bath. They will open all the rooms on that floor of the house. I heard her say they are renting chairs."

"Now why would any mother do that to her daughter?"

"Because she cannot conceive of failure."

"Well, I can. Vividly. You be in the front row and applaud passionately no matter what happens."

Once again the jovial doctor insisted on paying for Leighton's meal. Try as he might to cast him in the role of villain, Leighton could not make it stick.

As he lay in bed later, trying to sleep, Leighton wondered what motive Murray could have for betraying his country. Well, he was Flemish, so England wasn't his country. But he seemed to have plenty of money and enjoyed the social life of Bath. On the other hand, as a doctor, he could fit in anywhere.

Reid might have a motive, being placed on inactive duty since the war was over. He had endured much pain for his country, but he didn't need money either. He had an estate and title in his future. At least he said he had.

Gifford? No, too stupid even if he did need money. He would never endanger his future with Dierdra by selling out his country. It had to be someone else, whoever hid in Patience's salon. Just as he drifted off to sleep, the scent of tobacco came back to him vividly the way only scents can. There was a connection between Patience and the message, though a tenuous one. Perhaps he would discuss it with Maddie tomorrow, but carefully, very carefully.

Chapter Eighteen

Maddie had been up early to work through her pieces, and it was a good thing. The morning practice was twice interrupted by Lady Haddon measuring rooms, once by the men delivering the extra chairs, and finally by the seamstress working on Dierdra's dress. Maddie could see the girl being twisted into knots, and she did not like it. Maddie would be able to carry off her part, but Dierdra was green at this. Finally, at half-past eleven, the girl burst into tears.

Maddie sat beside her on the piano bench and supplied her with a handkerchief.

"Get your music, girls," Leighton said. "We are going into the garden to practice, unless your mother is planning on setting up a tent there for the overflow."

Dierdra gave a watery chuckle. "Will it be a disaster, Leighton?"

"Only if they run out of Champagne. Trust me, you will do fine. And once you conquer tomorrow, you will know in your own heart that if you practice well, you will always do fine." Leighton carried his cello to the remote bench and Maddie brought a music stand for him. He used the instrument to accompany the girls on the vocal pieces.

After they had practiced everything they could outside, Dierdra, though she could sing, still looked frightened. "This is the biggest event of my life," she said. "What if it is an utter failure?"

"Your life will be made up of a few big moments and many little ones," Maddie said. "The little moments are more important."

Dierdra smiled. "You are right. It will all be over soon and I will put it behind me whether it is a success or a failure."

They went in for lunch, and by then the chaos had died down enough for them to get to the pianoforte. But all the practice time was used by Dierdra. Maddie decided Leighton would look a fool if he was the only one not prepared. So she told him the room was his while she went to change for Patience's tea.

Leighton ran over his own composition a few times. It was short enough to know from end to end with no music in front of him. He was satisfied with it and nothing was more fatal than overdoing it. When Maddie came down the stairs, Dierdra was with her.

"Oh, good. Dierdra, are you going too?"

"Yes, we were all invited. Mother says she should not go since there is so much to prepare, but on the other hand…"

"She will get to brag about the affair in advance of it," Leighton guessed. "Maddie, does this mean Patience is part of the half of Bath who was invited?"

"Probably, but if we are all going to tea, there may not be an opportunity to ask my sister any questions." Maddie arched an expressive eyebrow at him.

Dierdra looked from one to the other of them in confusion, then started humming her solo as they made their way down the hill.

"That's right," Leighton said. "Practice in your mind if you cannot practice anywhere else."

They arrived after Mrs. Scope-Nevins, Dr. Murray, and Lady Haddon, who had come by carriage. These three were clustered around Patience as she presided over the tea table. There were also four other ladies there, whom Leighton recognized from the Pump Room. They occupied the comfy sofa, forcing Dierdra to occupy a chair by her mother, and Maddie and Leighton to perch on the window seat.

He leaned toward Maddie after they had been served and whispered, "Patience has deliberately invited a flock of people so she won't have to be alone with us."

"Well, Mrs. Scrope-Nevins is obviously not lurking in the second best salon."

"Someone is."

"It's no one, no one, I say. It's just your imagination, Leighton. And I let you worry me with your silly plots."

"That message wasn't a silly plot. You decoded it yourself."

"A mistake. It was meant for someone else."

"I checked. There was a Mr. and Mrs. Stone at the hotel, but they left days ago."

"It could have been for them. Where did they go?"

"I don't know. How much time do you think I have to ask questions with all this rehearsing?"

"Leighton, we are going to have to table our investigation until after tomorrow night."

"What if Lady Scope-Nevins and this unknown Stone don't table it? We cannot put the fate of our country after a silly musicale."

"It is not silly for Dierdra. It could ruin her with society if she freezes up."

"Yes, I know. And why am I arguing with you? We are on the same side."

"Leighton!" Lady Haddon demanded. "I asked what you are playing tomorrow night."

"It is an untitled composition."

"Ah, an original. Wonderful. Come, Dierdra. We cannot dawdle here all day. There is much to be done."

The hapless girl gave them a weak wave as she trailed out after her mother. Dr. Murray and the other ladies took their departure as a hint to leave. Mrs. Scope-Nevins was a little more dense, and Leighton could tell Patience was getting nervous. Finally, when all the teapots were empty and the trays of cakes had been reduced to crumbs, the woman left and Patience shut the door on her.

"I thought she would never leave. I do not know why I invite her."

"Perhaps to keep us from asking you any embarrassing questions?" Leighton suggested.

Patience sat and faced him, a slight color in her cheeks. "I am sure I can answer any questions you think to put to me."

"Why did you send me the packet of music with the message in it?"

"Music? I don't know what you're talking about. Why would I send you music?"

Maddie watched the deeper flush of crimson ascend her sister's cheeks and stood up. "You may as well tell us the truth, Patience. We are going to find out anyway."

Patience threw a nervous glance toward the closed double doors and pressed her hands to her cheeks. "It is better you do not know."

Leighton growled, stood up and strode toward the double doors, throwing them open—to be confronted by a man and a woman. Leighton blinked and a gasp was wrung from him as he stared at the two people rising from the sofa. The tall man with burnished russet hair was his father…and the woman was Maddie's mother.

"I should like to say I can explain, but I…" His father faltered.

The rest of his father's comment was lost in Leighton's embrace. When Leighton finally stepped back to look at the man, he saw the gray in the hair, the tiredness of the eyes that used to be so merry. "You are not dead! I am amazed. Your ship did not sink after all."

"No, I reached America without incident."

"It was you. You sent that scrap of music."

"The puzzle? Yes."

"Why didn't you just tell me you were alive?"

Mrs. Westlake peeked around them toward her daughters. Leighton heard Maddie gasp, and a teacup crashed to the floor. He turned to her with joy in his heart, but it was not happiness he saw in her face. She looked tragic.

"What does this mean?" Maddie asked, putting one hand to her throat. "How can this be? You are both dead."

"They are alive," Leighton said. "Be glad with me." He let loose of his father to go to Maddie, but she backed away and he feared she might faint. However, Maddie was not pale, a crimson flush suffused her face.

"Now I see. They have been together all this time."

"Yes, but it will be all right," Leighton assured her.

"But she left me. She left *me* to be with him." Maddie turned and ran from the room.

"Maddie, wait," Patience called.

"I must go after her," Leighton said, coming back a moment to clasp his father's hand again. "Promise me you will both stay right here."

Maddie had slowed to a rapid walk, only occasionally having to dash the tears from her eyes to see where she was going in her progress up the hill toward Marsden House. She had hoped not to call attention to herself. But the most casual observer would know she was distraught. How could her mother have done this to her?

"Maddie, wait," Leighton called as he strode after her. "You must come back."

"Why, to watch you make a fool of yourself?"

"But Maddie, you never even gave them a chance to explain."

"It is obvious. They ran off together, leaving us to carry on all the work."

"It does look that way, but we don't know, and they deserve to be heard." He took her arm and tried to turn her to look at him.

"Not by me. You inherited an earldom and all the power that goes with it. I had to scrape along as the vicar's daughter with no hope of a future." Her voice had dropped to an intense whisper. "What can she say to me, other than that she left me to be with her lover?"

"But Patience was living at home then. Your mother did not leave you alone."

"Well, that is the way it ended up." Maddie jerked out of his hold and continued her walk.

"I don't understand. I would trade everything to have my father back again. And he is back. It's a miracle. Why don't you even want to speak to your mother?"

"Because she put her own happiness before mine."

"But you spoke so kindly of your mother before, when you thought she was dead. We have them back again. Another chance. Do you know how rare that is?"

Maddie stared into his eyes. She saw the joy mixed with his sympathy for her and his total lack of understanding. "A mother's love should be unconditional."

Leighton bent his head toward her with that hard stare he used so seldom. "So should a daughter's."

"Don't you understand? She chose her *lover* over me. And if you persist in associating with them, then any notion of a marriage between us is off."

"Maddie," he pleaded, "I know this hurts you more because you were closer to Rachel than your sisters were. Your mother does love you. Why else would she have come back?"

"It's been too long. I've already mourned her. I can't let her back into my heart to hurt me again."

"Maddie." He whispered her name so faintly she had the illusion they were already separated by miles and years and emotions that could never be reconciled. "So you ask me to make the same choice. You're not being fair, either."

She turned her back on him and walked toward Marsden House. She did not know when Leighton stopped following her, but her one glance backward showed him standing in the street, with a pained expression on his face. The truth of his words hurt almost as much as the pain of seeing her mother. So he had made his choice and it wasn't her. Leighton was no better than her mother. Very well, she had lived without him before, and she could do so again.

Leighton returned to the house. To his relief, he found his father and Rachel Westlake having tea with Patience.

"I shall talk to her again tomorrow," he promised.

Patience poured him a cup and doctored it with cream and sugar. "I knew we shouldn't tell her."

Leighton sat down with a sigh. "She will see reason. It was just a shock. At least I am glad you are both alive, but what happened?"

His father glanced at Rachel, and she nodded. "Our relationship was platonic and would have remained so."

Rachel gave him a sad, kindly smile and said, "But every kindness your father did me drove my husband into fits of jealousy. Finally, one night while Maddie was up at the manor house, my husband accused me of having an affair and put me out of the house."

Patience stroked her mother's hand. "You had no choice but to leave then. I know what Papa is like."

"I would have had nothing but the clothes I stood in, if Patience had not packed a bag for me and sneaked out with it. She was the one to go to…William, for help."

"William?" Leighton asked.

"Yes, my new name," his father said. "I hitched a team myself and took Rachel to a hotel in Hereford. I decided separation was the only answer. I'm sure you were always aware that my marriage to your mother was a disaster. She was angry, but she agreed to mediate with the vicar. After Rachel spent three days in Hereford, your mother and the vicar finally came to terms."

"William and I were to move to America and never return to England. We agreed, packed, and left in the dark of night, planning to fight the legal battles later."

"And mother sold your horses," Leighton supplied with a tired sigh.

"Lord, no! I hired a brace of grooms in Hereford and took them with us."

"That's a relief." Leighton smiled to think of all

those beautiful horses still with his father, whom they loved. "So why didn't you get separated, Rachel? There is provision for that, when a husband is so cruel."

"The first ship that followed us carried letters from both my wife and her husband. They informed us of our *deaths*, trapping us on the other side of the Atlantic. They gave out that Rachel had died of a fever and I was lost at sea.

Patience sighed. "But I knew Mother was not dead and maintained a correspondence with her until the war started between England and America."

"Patience was already engaged to Carter," Rachel explained. "Maddie was supposed to live with Patience and her husband, not stay with her father. Don't you see? Westlake broke his word about so many things. My concern for Maddie has been driving me to distraction. I knew he would take all his anger out on her."

His father ran a hand through his hair. "With the war between England and American preventing travel, we didn't have much to hold onto except an occasional letter that slipped through on a neutral ship. Now that the world is more or less at peace, we booked passage on a ship bound for France. They left us on the Island of Guernsey and we made our way to Bath."

Rachel started to cry again. "What have I done? It was better when she thought me dead. Now I have wounded her twice."

"Do not give up on Maddie just yet," Leighton said. "She may be a passionate girl, but she usually does see reason."

"But my leaving made Maddie a prisoner, and she was alone with him."

"Still, you are back and everything will be as it was.

Well, perhaps not everything."

"You mistake matters," his father said. "We have no intention of disclosing our identities or remaining. We came only to see to your welfare and Maddie's."

"What about Susan and Amy?"

"You may tell Amy and Ross, and eventually Susan when you think she is old enough to know. Better yet, bring her to visit us in America."

"But you are the Earl of Longbridge, and I do not want to be," Leighton protested.

"After I *died*, I wrote a codicil to my will leaving your uncle William Stone the lands in Virginia."

"Yes, so the solicitors informed me. I didn't know I had an uncle— Oh, I see, *uncle*."

"Yes, poor William was born on the wrong side of the blanket, but in spite of his shady past, I have acknowledged him."

Leighton chuckled. "Are you sure about this?"

"I am content as things are, provided you will cross the Atlantic to visit us now and then."

"Of course we will, Maddie and I and Susan if we can manage it."

"You seem pretty confident about Maddie forgiving us."

"This is not the first time she has decided not to marry me. I am getting good at begging forgiveness."

"Oh, really? So you did manage to give her a disgust of you?" Patience asked, staring at him through her pince-nez. "What did you do?"

Leighton laughed. "For one thing, I suggested you were engaged in a clandestine affair."

"What?" Patience shrieked.

Rachel and William chuckled at her outrage.

"Then I thought perhaps you were involved in a spy ring."

"Now why would you think that?"

"That packet of music with the coded message. You sent it, didn't you, Father?"

"You are a fanciful boy, but yes, I sent it. Did you solve it?"

"I made a start, but Maddie found the solution."

Rachel smiled and his father nodded gravely. "Her intuition was always better than yours."

"And lastly, I speculated that Vicar Westlake may have murdered his wife and that you, Patience, were covering for him."

"Truer than you know," Rachel agreed. "He almost did kill my spirit."

"And I certainly did a lot of covering up," Patience said. "What now?"

"Maddie needs time to think this through. I will talk to her tomorrow. You are coming to this musicale?"

"I would not miss it," Patience said. "I hope to wrangle an invitation for my friends from America."

Leighton thought about his father's lack of appreciation for music and chuckled. "I look to see you there. But I rather hope Maddie does not, unless she becomes reconciled to the idea."

"We will be discreet," Rachel said.

They talked of the past then, the better moments of it. Leighton was so overjoyed to have his father restored to him that he was strolling home after supper and brandy before he realized he'd forgotten to delve further into the coded music, to ask if there was anything serious behind it. It was a joke, of course. His father would explain things tomorrow.

Chapter Nineteen

Maddie had known that, if she went to her room, Dierdra would be likely to rush in and interrupt her despair. She had been deeply hurt, and she just wanted to cry and punch things until the feeling went away. But she was not given to tantrums, so she thought no one would notice if she sat alone in the garden on a bench and wept, not even if she did so for hours.

"Dierdra, what is it?" Gifford's voice cut through the twilight as he tramped toward the house from the stables. "Oh, you are not Dierdra."

"Does she spend a great deal of time crying in the back garden?"

"She seems to cry for no good reason that I know of, and she isn't particular where she does it."

Maddie realized Gifford might be the reason for some of those tears, but he was too obtuse to understand.

"Well, I have a good reason."

Gifford sat on the bench beside her and heaved a sympathetic sigh. "And what is that?"

It was a relief to be able to talk to someone— anyone—about the injustice. "It's only that Leighton has betrayed me."

"Ah, I was not wrong then in thinking there was something between you and Stone."

Gifford rested his elbows on his knees. "So he is not after Dierdra."

"He never was, and I am alone now. Even my sister is against me."

Gifford nodded, a crease between his brows. "A sore trial for you. Do not think yourself abandoned. When Dierdra and I are married, there will always be a place in our household for you."

"Are you to be married?"

"Yes, well, we were until Stone's grand display of valor. Who would have thought I could be upstaged by a mere music master."

She prevented herself blurting out that Leighton was an earl. It was no longer her place to defend him. "He always was stupidly brave."

"Perhaps he meant to break with you because he's set his sights on Dierdra. Her parents are well-disposed toward him now that he has saved her life."

"But Leighton has been so careful to keep her from falling in love with him."

"If he is not interested in her, why did he insinuate himself into the Haddon household?"

"To be near me, of course."

"Sir Phillip has a prestigious position in Parliament. Is it possible Leighton is more interested in gaining his favor than you realize?"

"I don't think so. Leighton wants nothing to do with war or politics. He told me so." Her defense of Leighton would have carried more weight if she was not still so angry at him.

"He was making up to you as well as to Dierdra. Perhaps both of you were deceived in him."

"Perhaps." Her mind was too fogged with tears and regrets to think clearly, but it seemed Gifford was fishing for something and she did not want to say any more to him.

"Remember what I said. There will always be a place for you in my home."

He left her feeling not so much comforted as confused. Was Leighton, who saw spies under every couch, still working for the government and not telling her? There was plenty he had withheld until she'd wormed it out of him.

Or did he just wish to still be involved in the action and was using this opportunity to get into Sir Phillip's good graces? She shook her head.

No, the message was real, the accident was not staged, and Leighton had foolishly thrown his life into the balance in order to save a misguided but sweet girl. He had also ridden his favorite horse over a cliff for her.

But that was her Leighton, always acting on impulse without counting the cost to himself, at least not very carefully. He certainly never thought what effect it would have on Maddie. And he *had* insinuated himself at Marsden House to get close to her. Of that she was sure. So whatever Gifford was thinking sprang from his jealousy of Leighton's better qualities.

Better qualities? Yes, he forgave easily, and he apologized very well once he realized his error. But to forgive his father and her mother for such a crime? It was like losing them twice, and now she had lost Leighton as well. The tears flowed more freely now, with an occasional hiccup.

Looking around the garden, she realized she had come back here to think because this was where it had all gone awry, where Leighton had revealed his suspicions to her and then recanted them when he saw how upset she was. That had been a lie. He had still suspected Patience but took it back so as not to lose Maddie. And he had been right, in a way. Her sister was involved in a conspiracy, but not spying for another country. She should be glad Patience was not a traitor to anyone but her and her father.

Maddie tried to put herself in her sister's place six years ago. Would she have agreed to cover her mother's escape with a lie? Perhaps. Would she have abandoned a younger sister? *Never.*

There was another more uncomfortable question Maddie realized she had to ask herself. Was she angry because of the abandonment, or because she had not been trusted with the secret? Patience had treated her as badly as Leighton by thinking she could not handle serious matters. Maddie did not want to be shielded. She wanted them to acknowledge her competence.

In the uncertain light of the new moon, Leighton had trouble finding the gate to the walled garden at Marsden House, and when he did it was locked. He found a section of wall where the bricks had lost some of their mortar, got a toehold, and climbed over the six-foot impediment. He would have landed without incident but got tripped up by the ivy on the top and hit the ground with a loud thump and grunt.

"Who's there?"

"It's me, Maddie. I have to talk to you." He disentangled himself and limped toward the stone bench.

"How did you know I would be out here?"

"I didn't. I was going to throw rocks at your window."

Maddie looked almost ghostly in the bright white dress reflecting the moonlight. Perhaps she was pale, too.

"What is the use?" She stood up and watched him

warily. "You have taken their side against me."

He came up to her and tried to get an arm around her, but she moved to the other side of the stone bench and turned her back on him. He sat with a sigh. At least she had not run inside and locked the door.

"Leighton, I never imagined that something like this could happen. Does Papa know they are alive?"

"Well, of course he knows. He caused the whole mess. You should have stayed at your sister's house and let Father explain."

"And what other explanation can there be but that he ran away with my mother?"

"Passing themselves off as dead was not their idea. It was a plot cooked up by *my* mother and *your* father to save *their* faces."

She half turned toward him, and he could see the accusation on her face in the faint light from the window. "So what were they meaning to do?"

"Nothing. They had a friendship, and it would never have gone beyond that if it were not for your father's jealous accusations. They were unfounded at that point. But you know what he is like in a temper. On no grounds, he accused them of an affair. He put your mother out of the house."

"What? That never happened."

"Yes, it did. Your mother had no one else to turn to. Your father forced them together by giving your mother no choice. Father took her to a hotel and went back for his things, meaning to sail with Rachel to his lands in America and take care of the legalities of separation from their mates later. He felt badly that I was away at school and he could not tell me personally. Your father and my mother agreed to everything."

Maddie sniffed. "I don't remember any of that."

"Do you remember Patience coming for you at Longbridge and hustling you off to Faith's in York?"

"Yes, she sent me on the mail coach, but that was to protect me from the fever."

"There was no fever in the village, just the ague, what we always have during a wet summer. By the time Patience came for you, your father had set it about that your mother was dead. Since he is the one who lays out the dead, he could bury an empty coffin. When I got home, my mother announced my father had been lost at sea on the way to America. I never thought to doubt her word or check to see if a ship had gone down."

"How could they get away with such lies without the agreement of your father and my mother?"

"They were believed because no one makes up such tragic news and no one was there to refute them. Patience would have had to expose both of them publicly, and she was in no position to do that. She didn't even tell me."

"You cannot blame her. She wasn't married then."

"I know. She was still under your father's power, and he could be very convincing."

"I am not afraid of him." Maddie slid closer as though ready to fight an enemy.

"I have no doubt that if you had been the elder you would have exposed the plot and all would still be a messy scandal, but not so bad as it is."

"Yes, with them living together in sin."

"They are living under assumed names as man and wife, Mr. and Mrs. William Stone. Father has created an illegitimate but now recognized brother. And in my heart I feel he and Rachel belong together."

"You forgive them this misalliance?"

Her head came up, her chin proud. He was glad he could not see the anger in her eyes.

"Forgive them for finally finding someone capable of love? Yes, but I am so glad they are alive I would forgive them much worse than that."

"Well, I do not. They should not have fled."

"Your father threw her out. What was she to do, with no money and nowhere to go? My father was the only person who could help her."

Leighton could see her fists clenched beside the pale muslin of her dress, an incongruous vision of both strength and beauty, but that was Maddie. She was in shock and pain still, over what had happened.

"Why is it so much worse for a mother to have abandoned her daughter than for a father to leave a son? She was young, desperate and bereft. Father felt your mother had suffered enough."

"Suffered?" Maddie stood up as though ready to bolt. "Of all people, I should know what she suffered with my father. He is always picking, needling, condemning, even when you are doing your best, trying to avoid his razor tongue."

"Then you understand."

"I understand she let me think she was dead. She didn't trust me with the same truth that Patience was allowed to know. In that way she is much like you, who never trusted me."

"You are right that I betrayed you. I regret that more than you know. And I understand the pain you are feeling. But it wasn't supposed to be that way." Leighton got up slowly, realizing that if he had not betrayed Maddie's trust as well, she might not be so angry at her mother. "When Patience married, she was to take you with her or send you to Faith. That is what she promised your mother. In time, I think she would have told you the truth."

"Except that Papa talked Patience out of my living with her. That I do remember. Perhaps she never intended it, but Mother bought her freedom at the price of my enslavement." She folded her arms as though that was her final word.

"No." Leighton tried to drain the anger out of his own voice, but he would not let her go on deluding herself. "You have done that yourself by refusing to marry me."

"Free myself from my father only to be lorded over by you?"

Leighton stepped close enough to see the slow slide of a tear down her cheek in the moonlight. This was just a brave front. She was more hurt than he realized. "Maddie, I am not capable of that. You know I am not." He got close enough to fold her in his arms and felt a shudder go through her, but she did not weep, only sniffed and laid her cheek on his shoulder. "As it turns out, you were strong enough to face what drove your mother to despair. Can you not forgive her for not being able to endure your father as well as you did?"

She stayed like that for long minutes, breathing in and out with him holding her. Leighton almost thought he had won her back. But she raised her head to look at him.

"I need time. Leave me. I have to think."

He knew her well enough not to push her further, and he let his arms drop. He watched her float to the back door, a thin white wisp of a girl with moonlight in her hair. She turned but did not say anything before she disappeared in the door like a ghost. Had he killed her love for him by siding with his father?

He made his way to the gate this time. His ribs were still aching from falling over the wall, and he hated to face what his man would say about his scuffed boots and snagged shirt. But nothing compared to the ache he felt for Maddie. If she really made him choose between her and his father, he was not sure what he would do.

****

"Been climbing trellises again, have we?" Tibbs asked.

Leighton sat bolt upright in bed. The sun was shining in the window, where Tibbs had brutally swept the hangings aside. Leighton groaned as he crawled out of bed. "No, it was a stone wall."

"Ah, that explains it."

Leighton limped to the washstand and splashed water on his face. "Tibbs, aren't you going to rant at me?"

"Well, I have been this past hour, but you slept through it. Waste of breath. Are you wishing to go out today?"

Tibbs draped a dressing gown over Leighton's shoulders. He stuck his arms in the sleeves and seated himself at the round table in the sitting room. He could smell tea and really needed some.

"Yes, what time is it? I have to give another music lesson. The recital is tomorrow night."

"First you'll have yer breakfast."

As Leighton ate, he wondered about the change in his man. Had Dr. Murray told him about the episode on the cliff? Something had softened him, and Leighton was not sure he liked it. It was rather nice having someone around who did not approve of him.

As Tibbs helped him dress, Leighton saw his gaze fasten on the newly bruised ribs on the other side of his chest and on the fresh scrapes.

"You said you was done with the spying business."

"This had nothing to do with that."

"When I agreed to leave London, you promised that there would be no more excitement."

"I know. I am sorry. But once I win Maddie, how often will I have to crawl over a wall? I promise you that our lives, from the day of my wedding on, will be suitably dull."

"Good. That will save wear and tear on your clothing."

Leighton went to Marsden House and checked on the horses. Jasper was filling out well and Chandros was eager for a run. He felt his own ribs. Perhaps tomorrow.

Leighton was admitted through the back door and shown to the drawing room. He immediately began to play, knowing that would draw Maddie if she was in the house and willing to speak to him.

"You have a lot of nerve coming here," Maddie said from behind him, her voice vibrating with hurt.

Leighton stopped playing and turned to her. She was standing by the sofa but with no apparent intention of taking a seat, so he rose and went to her. "I had to talk to you. I thought your heart might have softened toward them."

"Leighton, how can you expect me to accept them after what they did?"

"The reason they came back is that your mother was worried about you. Now she is devastated since she thinks she has made things even worse."

"*She* is devastated?"

"I remember now how sad she always looked at home, though she tried to hide it. I think her happiness with my father can never make up for her feeling of failure with you."

"I'm-I'm sorry to disappoint you, Leighton, but I cannot see her again. It hurts too much."

"Think about it, Maddie. They will be here only a few months until a ship can take them back to America."

"I cannot change my mind. What I don't understand is how you forgive so easily."

"I try not to judge people. I have enough trouble keeping myself straight. But then I'm not the child of a vicar, so perhaps my morals are a little rustier. At least now we know your sister is not harboring a spy."

"That was a silly idea."

Leighton began to hope that Maddie would rebound with her usual strength. At least she had slept last night, for her eyes, though sad, were not shadowed by circles. She was getting over it, or getting used to it.

"Yes, I am good at looking silly to you. I suppose this means you won't play for us at the musicale."

She hesitated. Then her chin came up. "I have been promised a position in Gifford's household once he marries Dierdra, so yes, I will play."

Leighton recognized the remark for what it was, a ploy to irritate him. "If I stop coming to Haddon House—leave the field, so to speak—Dierdra won't marry someone nice like Lieutenant Reid. She will be forced to make do with Gifford, the pompous ass."

"He doesn't think much of you either, Leighton. That message your father sent…"

"It must have been a joke. He sent it to me because

he wanted to see if I—we—could still solve his riddles."

"But it referred to Mrs. Scrope-Nevins. How did he know about her?"

"I don't know. We didn't discuss it. Patience must have mentioned her in a letter. She did write to them by posting mail via ships from neutral countries."

"So why was she at the tea? What exactly did your father say about the packet?"

"I don't know. We got so busy talking I forgot to ask about it."

"You forgot?" Her voice was pregnant with derision.

"Yes, it's funny. I had once or twice thought I saw someone familiar on the streets. It is just the sort of game he would play. And the scent on the paper was tobacco smoke. I had smelled it in your sister's house, but it didn't register that it was his."

"Why would it? You thought he was dead. Don't you see, Leighton? He got the packet from someone and thought it was an amusing puzzle, so he sent it *on* to you. It is a *real* coded message, not something he made up. He is the Stone they were trying to contact, and they succeeded. It's your father who is the spy, not my sister."

"What? That is the most absurd—"

"Not so funny when the shoe is on the other foot, is it?" She stood with hands on hips, waiting for his reply.

"Come now, Maddie. He may be living in America, but he would never stoop to conspiring against our government."

"It makes more sense than—"

As he heard Dierdra's feet on the stairs, Maddie backed away from him and pretended to be searching through the pile of music scores.

"I have decided what to wear," Dierdra announced.

"Not the new dress, which isn't ready, but my favorite dress. It is more comfortable for breathing. Do you think Dr. Murray and Lieutenant Reid will come?"

Maddie nodded. "I am sure they were invited. You haven't changed your mind again about what you are going to play, have you?"

"Oh, you are right. 'The Moonlight Sonata,' of course. Did you hear me practicing last night?"

"No, I was…not feeling well."

Dierdra came to take her hands. "I hope it is nothing serious. Will you be able to play tomorrow?"

"Yes, of course. Now practice for Leighton. He is the best judge of how ready you are."

By the time Dierdra got to the end of the sonata, Maddie realized Mrs. Marsden was sitting in the room listening. She was in her bonnet and shawl, so she was obviously on her way to the Pump Room to gossip with her friends. Leighton had kept track of where Dierdra had stumbled slightly and made her play those parts over until they were perfect. Then he made her promise to practice the piece twice through again that night. The rehearsal of the vocal numbers went without a hitch, so Maddie started to get optimistic about the coming recital.

"Well, child, are you looking forward to tomorrow?" Mrs. Marsden asked Dierdra.

"Oh, yes, but I need new ribbons for my blue dress."

"On our way back from the Pump Room. Leighton, will you walk with us? Maddie, are you coming?"

"Yes, of course." Anything would be better than staying here and continuing to argue with Leighton, though she rather thought she had won the last round, since he was looking thoughtful. Accusing his father of being a spy should have made her feel better, but it did not. It had hurt Leighton. Was that what marriage was like, hurting each other until the mounting emotional pain drove you apart? But when Leighton blurted out something stupid, it was accidental. She had deliberately wounded him. She had not thought she could be so vengeful.

"What is the sequence of the numbers?" Mrs. Marsden asked as Leighton took her arm and they went down the hill to the Pump Room.

"First is the piano solo from Dierdra."

"Yes, I want to get that over with," the girl said.

"Then a long duet, with me on the cello and Maddie on the piano, a ballad with Dierdra singing and Maddie playing, a short composition from me, and as an encore piece, a duet from the girls with me playing the pianoforte."

Maddie spoke up to veto the last, claiming her voice was not good. So they substituted Maddie on the piano.

"I suppose we should think of a second encore piece," Maddie said.

"No need," Mrs. Marsden replied. "Several of the company can play, and I will coerce them into it. One of them is your sister Patience. Look, there she is now."

Maddie sucked in her breath, for her mother and Leighton's father were with Patience. Leighton turned to her, a pleading look on his face. She found herself stepping forward with the rest of the party.

"Well met, Mrs. Carter. I hope you still plan to come to our musicale tomorrow night."

"Yes, I never miss a chance to hear good music."

Maddie could see Patience's face was flushed.

"Who are your friends?"

"Allow me to present William Stone and his wife,

Rachel, visiting from America. This is Mrs. Marsden and her granddaughter, Dierdra Haddon, and—and—"

"Stone? Any relation?" Mrs. Marsden asked.

"Yes," Leighton said, stepping forward and embracing his father. "My uncle. Well met again after so many years."

He kissed Rachel on the cheek and hugged her. Maddie felt tears well in her eyes, but she swallowed them and avoided eye contact with her mother.

"You are probably acquainted with Miss Westlake, as well," Mrs. Marsden said.

"We have met," Maddie said in a rush, ducking her head in acknowledgment.

"Patience, you must bring them with you Saturday. I cannot have you abandoning your guests."

"Oh, no," Rachel said with a blush. "We cannot impose on you."

"Nonsense. It's but a recital to flaunt the talents of these young people. Please, I want you there. Say you will come."

Maddie saw Leighton nodding to his father and that made her angry. How was she supposed to play with such overwhelming emotions roiling in her breast?

"Very well, we would love to attend," Rachel said. "It has been a long time since I have heard Miss Westlake play, and I have sorely missed it."

The kindness and affection in Lord Longbridge's eyes broke something in Maddie's heart, and she gulped. She sucked in a breath and looked at her mother, who was trembling. Why did everything always depend on her? She lifted her chin. "Yes, it has been many years since I played at all. 'Tis a wonder I have not forgotten all that I knew."

"That's all settled then," Mrs. Marsden replied.

After a few more pleasantries, Leighton offered to walk them home. He had started up the hill with them when Maddie turned on him.

"No need to make the trip up the hill again today, Leighton. We will see you in the morning."

He looked at her with pain in his eyes. She wanted to embrace him, to say how sorry she was, but apologizing was supposed to be his job. The fault was his, not hers, wasn't it? He had what he wanted. She had recognized her mother without shouting at her. More she could not give. But his eyes were so like his father's, kind and understanding behind the hurt.

Leighton went back to his hotel. He had just made it to the lobby when he saw Lieutenant Reid, who appeared to be registering.

"Coming over to stay at Prad's? Have lunch with me in the courtyard."

"Very well."

The man came out and sat at the table Raymond held for Leighton. He seemed unaffected by the sunshine, the tinkling spring, or the gentle breeze that slipped through the dogwood trees. He asked for Madeira with his lunch and ate with military precision.

"You seem to have recovered from your adventure," Reid said.

"So has Dierdra. What's more, Sir Phillip seems to have stamped on Gifford's pretensions."

"Ah, I see. His star falls and yours rises." Reid tipped his glass in acknowledgment.

"But I do not want it to. I am in Bath for one reason and one only, to convince Maddie Westlake to marry me."

Reid resumed his chewing without looking up. "So you said."

"I do own to a ready sympathy for Dierdra and wonder if, without Maddie propping her up, she might be compelled into the disaster of marrying Gifford."

"Why would Miss Westlake leave?"

"She comes of age in a few days. If she hasn't washed her hands of me by then, I hope to make her my wife. If Dierdra had a choice of suitors…"

"I am quite sure she has many."

"Admirers. She needs someone who is serious about her. Someone with a future, with an estate and a title someday, for instance."

"Don't look at me so pointedly. I feel sorry for the girl too, but I have a job—"

"Oh, I thought you were on leave."

Reid took a deep breath. "Thank you for the lunch. I am sure I will see you again soon."

"You have been invited to Marsden House tomorrow night. If aught goes wrong with this musicale, Dierdra could use some friends in attendance."

Reid stared at him, then nodded and limped away.

Leighton still did not know if his claims to a title and land were false or real, but he did know there was a smoldering interest in Dierdra under the well-banked fires of Reid's passion. But what was he passionate about? Leighton began to believe Reid was here to look for the spy rather than sell out his country. Hence his interest in Dr. Murray and Leighton Stone.

He had no doubt that if Reid thought Leighton's father was in some kind of plot, he would have him arrested (or shoot him to save the trouble). What had the message said? *Will know location of fleet. Getting ships in train. Do you back enterprise? S-N.*

And how was the reply to be sent? This was not the first exchange of messages, so the recipient must have a way of responding. Leighton would give anything to know what the answer had been and who it had come from.

It did not really implicate his father, even if he was now an American. Mrs. Scrope-Nevins had lined up the ships to rescue Napoleon and wanted to know the location of the fleet but she didn't know it yet. That meant there was someone else involved. Were they asking his father for money?

He overturned his empty glass when he recalled what Dr. Murray had said. Sir Phillip had to do with the naval appropriations. He might know where the fleet was. Poor Dierdra, again.

Chapter Twenty

After sleeping on the problem, Leighton decided the wisest course was to ask his father if he had any involvement with a spy ring. He had the experience of people laughing in his face so often that it would not come ill from his own father. Why would he have sent the message on to Leighton as a joke if it was not trivial? If it turned out that he was involved, Leighton would just have to get him out of it.

On his way to Marsden House, he called at Patience's town house but no one was home. He had the feeling the butler was telling the truth this time. Leighton left a card for Mr. Stone on which he scrawled, "I must speak with you in private." He would see him tonight after the musicale, if not before.

Dierdra was already practicing when Leighton got to Marsden House, and she made it creditably through her piece. Her grandmother would have nothing to blush for in her performance. Today her mother sat through the rehearsal, with everyone playing the whole way through all the numbers. She suggested a slight rearrangement of the program and left them.

"I am exhausted," Dierdra said and stretched her arms. "How often must I practice the piece today?"

"Once only," Leighton said. "Don't give yourself a disgust of it."

"Very well. I am going to see if my maid has my

dress ready."

"Oh, Lieutenant Reid is back in town. I think we will see him tonight."

"Really? And his friend the doctor too, I'm sure."

When she had left them alone, finally, Maddie rose from her chair and glared at Leighton. "You're playing matchmaker now? With your lack of social adroitness?"

"I swear I did not know we would meet them in the Pump Room. But they cannot closet themselves in Patience's drawing room for three months. You must get used to seeing them." Leighton got off the piano bench and walked around behind her.

She set the music scores in the new order of play. "If you noted, I did not cause a scene."

"No, I was very impressed with how you handled what must have been a trying situation." He put his hands on her shoulders from behind and she did not elbow him in the ribs. That was a good sign.

"You were shaking in your boots," she said with her usual frankness.

"Only fearful that Rachel might break down." He rested his face next to her. "I knew I could count on you."

"It was your father who convinced me I must act the lady. He is no different, as sweet and kind as ever. You would hardly think he could have stolen another man's wife."

"I told you it wasn't like that," he whispered. "Your father's jealousy drove her away. Recall he locked your mother out of the house. What was she to do?"

"So you said, several times. But just because Lord Longbridge is your father doesn't make him perfect. He could have helped my mother get to York. He ruined my mother's life and mine."

"Once Westlake turned her out, though innocent, she would have been branded an adulteress no matter where she went in England."

"But I lost her for all those years."

"Had you known she was alive, would your father have given you leave or the money to go and visit her?"

"No, I suppose not."

"Your father ruined his own life by being so mean and jealous. You are not the only victim here. He drove your mother away with his unjust accusations, rages, and suspicions. Who could take such treatment?"

"I did." She looked sideways at him, a challenge in her fine green eyes.

"I know, and I am sorry for it. If I'd had any idea what you were going through, I would have abandoned my work and come back to help you."

"By marrying me?"

Leighton wrapped his arms around her, careful to walk the fine line between affection and possessiveness. "How else can I help except by putting all I have in your hands?"

"I never resented taking care of your people. It was being taken for granted that bothered me."

Leighton hugged her tighter. "I know now how much I erred, how it must have seemed to you. I should have told you what I was up to on one of my visits home. I should have contrived a way to meet you. You would never have let it slip to anyone."

"So you did appreciate what I did?"

"I did not see how I could do without you. I know it is difficult to forgive a betrayal as close as your own mother. My mother said something to me the last time she hugged me, that I must have more of a care with my life."

"That is all too true."

"She said I must do so because everything depended on me. If anything were to happen to me, they would be on the street."

Maddie turned in his arms to look at him. "That's all you mean to her?"

"Yes, but she is a shallow person, and I've always known that."

"So I should forgive your father and my mother because they are not shallow? They still betrayed me by not confiding in me."

"As your father did and as I did."

"And now Patience has, too." Maddie shook her head in amazement.

"Ask yourself why Patience forgave them."

Her gaze searched his face. "Why?"

"Love, Maddie. Love makes nothing else matter."

She shook her head again, compressing her lips. She was definitely dewy-eyed this time.

"Love cannot fix this."

Leighton raised a hand to brush a tear from her cheek. "Silly me. I thought love could fix anything. So you still mean to make me choose between you?"

She jumped a little in his arms. She had not been thinking that was what she had demanded of him. She felt her heart throbbing in her chest as though it was trying to escape her. She thought of the look of hope on his father's face, her own mother's mute, tearful appeal, and finally of Leighton. They had all hurt her, but none of them had meant it, and they all wanted forgiveness. Was that so hard a thing?

"No, my love for you does not depend on you not

making a fool of yourself." He pulled her down on the piano bench and she rested her head on his chest.

"A good thing, too, since I do it so often."

"So," Dierdra said from the doorway. "I was not mistaken about your intentions."

Maddie lifted her head to stare at her and Leighton looked up.

"Wait, let me explain," Leighton said, fearing a temper tantrum.

Dierdra looked smugly from one to the other of them. "I suspected there was something between you two from the start."

"Then you do not mind?" Maddie asked.

"No, not so long as you stop crying and get on with it. How can I focus on my playing or my future when you two are unsettled? Well, have you made up?"

"Yes," Leighton said, looking back at Maddie. "Unless I manage to blunder again."

"To prevent that, we would have to keep you locked in a cabinet until the wedding day," Dierdra said. After her parting shot, her tiny feet pounded back up the stairs. Leighton hugged Maddie and kissed her. His kiss was different now. It had more than the eager passion of a young man trying to woo. It now held the tenderness of a man who wanted a lifetime with her. She knew now, since they had survived this crisis, nothing but death could part them again.

****

Leighton was not reassured to discover that his father had ridden to Bristol that day. If one were making arrangements for ships or paying for those arrangements, Bristol would be the place to go.

Through Raymond, the footman at Prad's, he also

discovered that Dr. Murray had moved into the hotel the same day he had and had specifically asked for a room next to his. And Raymond was thinking of getting married himself, since he'd had a sudden influx of guineas from Leighton. Wonderful.

Tibbs was back to his usual acerbic self, asking how many times a week he was going to have to press and mend Leighton's evening suit. He sent him off with the warning not to go wall-crawling in his good shoes.

Leighton arrived to find that Maddie had worked her magic. She had the servants bustling about with punch bowls and chairs. He decided he was underfoot and went out the back door to the stables to visit his horses, hoping he would not step in anything before the big moment.

He'd ridden Chandros that morning without his ribs suffering and planned to take Jasper out tomorrow. When he walked back along the stalls, he found Gifford feeding bites of carrot to his Andalusian. It unnerved him.

"Quite a horse. I thought surely he would die after plunging over that cliff."

"Frankly, so did I." Leighton stroked the velvet muzzle and flattered himself that the horse preferred his attentions even though he didn't have any carrots.

"What do you want for him?"

"I am afraid I cannot sell him. He was a gift from a friend. He would never understand if I did. Besides, Chandros is to be the sire for my brood mares. If you would like a colt out of him, there I can oblige you."

"I would have to wait four years," Gifford complained.

"Some of the best things in life are worth waiting for."

"I have been waiting for Dierdra half my life."

220

"But she is only seventeen, not yet out."

"But I am eight and twenty. High time I settled down."

Leighton was tempted to ask if it was not better to give Dierdra a chance to choose for herself, but he had a notion Gifford would not like to hear that. And he would trust Maddie had trained Dierdra toward independence. One thing he could do was disarm the man. He obviously was trying to stake a claim. Leighton could truthfully say he wanted none.

"My mother has been badgering me to marry these five years, hence my pursuit of the fair Maddie."

"Miss Westlake, a parson's daughter? But they say you are an earl."

"But our attraction is of long standing, and we mean to marry no matter how many rubs are thrown in our way."

"So it was the Westlake chit you were after all along."

"Why, yes, what did you think?"

"You know damned well what I thought." Gifford stalked away. Leighton finally reached into his pocket for the lumps of sugar he had brought from the hotel. While he was talking to the horses, a small lad tugged at his coattail and handed him a letter. It had no salutation, so he asked the boy who it was from.

"I dunno, sir. The servant just said to find Mr. Stone, that he'd be at Marsden House tonight, said the butler would take it to him. Piece of luck you being in the stables."

The child had made his own luck, knowing Mr. Stone would give him more largess than a butler. Leighton put a coin into the boy's hand and watched him run off, then cracked the seal on the note.

Leighton groaned. It was in code. He stared at the brief score of music and started deciphering based on Maddie's decoding. It took him some minutes to substitute for each character and then order them in his mind.

Meeting arranged for courtyard at midnight. And that was all there was.

The message had the same feeling as the other one, but no scent of tobacco, so it definitely had not passed through his father's hands. Someone had gotten the wrong Stone this time. He folded the note and shoved it and the envelope into his pocket.

Even if the first note had been a jest, this was the real thing. Had his father sent him the previous message because he wanted out? Was it a plea for help? The only useful bit of information in this one was the time. When he thought of courtyard, the hotel came to mind. But it was highly unlikely to be the one that was meant. Still, if he finished up here before midnight, he would go in place of his father. He would find out what was going on, finally.

The thought that there might be danger did occur to him. He could be arrested as a spy, or shot, depending on how edgy Reid was feeling. So he went to the library and outlined the situation in a letter to Scoville, omitting any mention of his father. He folded it and prepared another letter to Maddie. But what was he to say to her? If there was danger, he did not want her involved. He did not even want to suggest he might be killed. In the end, he said that if there was a need for her to clear his reputation, the enclosure would do it.

Then he stopped to think about what position she

might be in if he was killed, so he wrote a will leaving everything he could to her and sealed that inside the letter to Scoville. It was inadequate protection for her, but it was something. The note to her ended with his undying love for her. It would never die even if he did.

Finally he went to put it in her room. If anything happened to him, at least his name would be cleared. He had a sudden vision of Maddie back at the parsonage, and his distant cousin putting up with his whining mother at Longbridge Keep. The saddest part was thinking of Maddie alone.

When Maddie finally saw Leighton, she was still arranging the music stands. "I thought you were going to come early. Is anything the matter?"

"No. What could be wrong?" He came up and pressed her hand and kissed it.

He seemed in an odd mood. "Leighton, you have a talent for understatement. This evening could be a disaster."

"You are always like this before a performance. I had thought it was because your father is such a perfectionist."

"Yes, you are right. I must calm myself so I do not make Dierdra nervous."

"You will see. We have not lost our edge, at any rate. Everything will be fine." He patted her hand and let go of it.

"Oh, by the way, Reid is here." She sent him a calculating look.

"I thought he might be."

"And Dierdra has suddenly remembered his heroics that day and is thanking him profusely."

"How is he taking that, being the knight in shining

armor for a change?"

"He actually blushed, but I fancy he is not indifferent to her."

Leighton wandered toward the refreshment table to inspect it. "You were accusing me of matchmaking. Did you have a hand in this case of hero worship?"

"I did point out that, had you not knocked her off her horse, Lieutenant Reid would have ridden to her rescue and taken her up across his saddle, carrying her off to safety. Leighton, stop eating those cakes. They are for the guests."

Leighton was staring at her with his mouth agape. "She swallowed that?"

"Yes, she is quite sure now that you only got in the way, and she knows in her heart that Gifford would never have lifted a finger to help her."

"Poor Dierdra. She has the right of it there. If it's romance she craves, Gifford is the worst possible husband for her."

"I do not think she will settle for him now. Oh, here come the first guests. I do not know if I can do this, not with *them* in the audience."

"You've played for my father and your mother dozens of times. This is no different."

Leighton watched Maddie nod her agreement, but her face was still pale. She had a good twenty minutes to regain her composure since it took that long for all the guests to find seats and rid themselves of greetings and gossip. Leighton went to reassure Rachel and Patience that all was well.

He drew his father aside. "That scrap of music you sent me was a jest, as you said?"

"Yes, what makes you ask?"

"Another message has come my way, and I think it is not in jest. It speaks of a meeting of conspirators at midnight and, unless I miss my guess, there will be a representative from the army there to arrest them."

"Are you sure it was intended for you?" his father asked calmly.

"Of course not. I think it was intended for you, and I am guessing it was sent by Sir Phillip, but I cannot prove it."

Lady Haddon was describing the night's entertainment and was about to turn the program over to Leighton.

His father patted him on the back and pushed him toward the front of the room. "Make me proud."

Proud of what? Capturing a spy ring or entertaining a throng of guests, at least one of whom was tone deaf?

"I have it on good authority that you…" Leighton stopped before he blurted out his father's flaw. Why cheat him of the pretext of enjoyment?

"What?"

"That you have musicians in America just as fine as we are."

"We are no backwater. Still, it has been a long time."

Mrs. Marsden called for attention and introduced the three of them. Dierdra began her piece as coyly as Leighton had taught her and was not a bit distracted by him turning the pages for her. The first two sections were slow, so she surprised everyone with the energy she expressed in that last part. It was the more technically complex but had been the simplest for Dierdra to master. Her fingers danced over the keys like fluttering birds, and Leighton felt a small thrill that he had helped her just a little to this moment of triumph. Every such victory a woman gained meant that she might stand up a little more valiantly for her own rights. Fifteen minutes later she was nodding modestly at genuine applause.

Lady Haddon had wanted Leighton's piece next, so he launched into his latest composition. It was perhaps a bit startling, part of it sounding as though it cataloged a pursuit on horseback and part as though he was accompanying a waterfall, but he was beyond looking for acceptance of his work. If only Maddie understood that it was for her. He had worked on it since that stumbling beginning all those days ago in the courtyard of the hotel when he did not even know if he was looking for her in the right city. He looked up as she turned the handwritten music for him and smiled at her.

She looked startled. She must have realized he didn't need the music. The notes were written on his heart. But constant, reliable Maddie went on turning the pages at the right moments anyway, miraculously reading the music upside down and watching his fingers on the keys as though observing the hands of a lover, deft, gentle, sure of his welcome. Was that last blush for him? What a public place in which to declare his love for her, and what a unique way.

He would have to ask her later if she understood what his hands were saying to her. The audience had been totally silent for Dierdra's Beethoven. Now he could hear an occasional whisper. That didn't surprise him. They could never have heard anything like this before and probably never would again. The bridge was slower, like a gently moving stream, swirling a boat with two lovers in it, oblivious to where the current was taking them, even if they drifted clear to the sea.

For the last section, the rider was back. No, two

riders, he and Maddie side by side, riding away to Longbridge forever. After the final chord there was a moment or two of silence. Then bold hands began clapping. Leighton looked up to see his father standing to applaud, and first one, then another of the audience following suit. Eventually all were persuaded to give him a hand, though he suspected many had not liked what they'd heard.

Without a break except for Maddie to take her place at the pianoforte and for him to tune his cello, they began a slow adagio, the only sad part of the program. Dierdra had been well coached on when to turn Maddie's pages, and Leighton could look over her shoulder if he needed to see the music. Dierdra sent him a delighted smile. He just hoped nothing would happen to ruin the evening for her—such as her father being arrested.

All things considered, Maddie was holding up rather well. As he had foretold, when she began to play, she forgot who was listening. For his own part, it was easy to carry those long notes that tied together the piece and gave it continuity. It was a difficult one to master on the piano, but Maddie had managed it.

He thought over all their recent misunderstandings and arguments, afraid that he would have no chance to speak to her before he had to try to avert this new disaster. He had made so many missteps in life it was amazing that she still wanted him.

He had been drafted out of university by a contact who knew Scoville was looking for someone. When he had gone off to help with the decoding, he'd no idea how big a dent he would make in her life. Now that he was back, he was not going to let anyone hurt her ever again, unless something dire happened in the next few hours.

Then it hit him. He should have told her, confided in her. This was just the sort of mock heroics that made her so angry at him. Well, it was not too late to confess this time, but he did not want her there with him, did not want to have to worry about her life as well.

Maddie paused, breathless after the last note. She thought they had never sounded so well together. Yes, they had played this piece before, but they had both been children then. Now she understood what perfect accord meant, for she had just experienced it. If they could agree so sweetly with their music, why could they not always be harmonious?

Leighton took her hand and lifted her, subtly turning her to face the audience. She looked down at her gray silk gown, trying to avoid her mother's eyes because she did not want to cry, but it was the false Mrs. Stone who was crying. Maddie sent her a sad smile. Perhaps Leighton was right. Perhaps his father and her mother belonged together and deserved each other. She looked at the way Lord Longbridge's hand covered her mother's, and she harked back to those visits he had made to the parsonage. Those were the only times she remembered her mother laughing.

Next was a light operatic piece, with Dierdra singing the soprano and Leighton the tenor. Maddie had never realized before how good Leighton's voice was. She worried for a moment about his cough, but he would not have attempted the short piece if he had not rid himself of that. And they were both strong enough to sing together without drowning each other.

When she turned to join Dierdra in the next ballad, she noticed Lieutenant Reid in the first row, watching them raptly. He seemed to be dividing his attention equally among the three of them, yet when he glanced at Dierdra his gaze was not keen and piercing. His eyes held a softer light, one that could be turned to love if the girl so desired and had the opportunity.

And she might. Dierdra's cool, clear voice was causing that beautiful smile on her father's face and the glint of pride in her mother's eyes. If she set her mind to it, the girl could have anything she asked for. Maddie would have to remember to point that out to her.

Dierdra's vocal solo with Maddie on the piano and Leighton on the cello finished the evening. When the last bars ended with the high, delicate, untouchable note dying away, there was a worshipful silence for a moment, then the bedlam of applause, talk, and the scrape of chairs. Maddie flattered herself that the audience had not been bored but were sincere in their enjoyment. Dierdra's parents both kissed her. Gifford gave up trying to approach her and left the room in sullen silence.

Leighton whispered something in Maddie's ear.

"What?"

"Your mother. Will you speak to her?"

"Oh, Leighton. I will cry if I do."

"No one will think aught of it."

"You ask too much. I cannot."

"Then just smile, something to let her know there is forgiveness in your heart, even if you cannot express it yet."

Maddie ducked her head, then glanced at the chairs of the new Mr. and Mrs. Stone and realized what they had given up to be together. Their whole lives, children, everything—and not by choice. She licked her lips and dashed a tear from her eyes—and sent her mother a brave smile.

She started across the room but was swept up in a crowd congratulating her. When she looked up again, they were gone.

"It was enough," Leighton said. "You made her very proud."

"I think I understand them better now, through you. I want to see her again."

"I hope so, for you may have to. I have an errand to run. It has to do with the business of the code. I do not know what it is all about yet, except that Reid is on the right side, I am sure."

Maddie felt her lips tremble. "You are just not sure your father is."

"Correct. I tried to talk to him tonight, but he avoided the issue."

"What can you do?"

"Go in his place. If anything should happen, I have written out what I know and left it on your pillow. Send the packet to Scoville or even Wellington. He is still in London."

"But Leighton, if you don't know what you are walking into, how can you defend yourself?"

"Don't worry. I shall come off all right. You'll see."

"Leighton, this is not a musical performance. This is real. It's a matter of your life, our life together."

"You are asking me to choose again, my father or you, and I want you both safe and sound. If anything should happen, go to him and tell him why I did it."

"But where are you going?"

"Where it all began…the message, the music." His eyes were glittering with excitement. "I wrote it for you. Did you guess? The new piece is called 'Constance

Madeline.' "

"Leighton, wait," she called after him as he escaped through the crowd.

Chapter Twenty-One

Maddie ran up the steps to her room. He had done it again, cast himself in the role of a stupid hero when he didn't even know the risks. Leighton did indeed need a keeper. She threw open her door and grabbed the note from her bed, ripping it open. It said nothing, or more of the same drivel he had been spouting. If he really loved her, he would not do such things. She had no compunction about tearing open the inner note as well, but it did not give the time or place of the meeting. When she came to his will, she felt a frisson of fear. Leighton would never have penned this if he did not believe in the danger.

"I'll take that, Miss Westlake."

Maddie jumped as Reid whisked the papers out of her hands and mastered them.

"When and where?" he demanded.

"I wish to God I knew. I would take a pistol and go shoot Leighton myself to put him out of his misery."

"But he is not involved. He was a suspect once, but we are sure of him now."

"Who are we?" she asked through gritted teeth.

"There is no time for that now," Reid said desperately. "Have you no idea where he may have gone?"

"The time has to be soon. As for where, all he said was 'where it all began.' He must have been talking about the first message he got, and that was delivered to his hotel."

"Stay here." Reid thrust the papers back in her hands. "I will do what I can to keep him safe."

"But what if you—"

He was gone. Just like a man.

She paced back and forth, trying to remember exactly what Leighton had said. Surely the meeting was not to happen in his room.

A knock on her door brought her up short, and then it was thrust open.

"Lady Haddon, is something the matter?"

"Could you come to the study, please?"

"Is it Dierdra? Is she ill?"

"No, Dierdra is fine. My husband must speak to you."

Maddie followed Dierdra's mother down the back stairs and entered a room in total disorder. It looked as though it had been ransacked, though she was pretty sure Reid had not done it. "Sir Phillip, what is it?"

"Did you see anyone enter the study this evening?"

"I was in the drawing room all evening. I can see the door from the front of the room, but not when I am playing. Are you saying someone took something?"

"Yes, my notes are missing."

"Notes?"

"From an important meeting with the Admiralty. I can say no more."

Maddie sat down, sending her mind back to that message that had come through Leighton's father, *Will know location of fleet.* For a second she doubted Lord Longbridge. Was he going to lead his own son into a trap with his machinations? But he would never hurt

Leighton. There must be some other explanation.

"You look as though you know something about this," Sir Haddon said gruffly.

Maddie's mind scrambled. She could not give Leighton's father away even if he was involved in this tangle somehow. "It was just something odd that happened to Leighton tonight."

"What?"

"A note had been misdirected to him, something about a meeting. Just like him not to tell me where."

"Are you sure the note was not intended for Leighton?"

"He did not think so. It was handed to him in the stable, where no one would think to look for him." Maddie thought again of what Leighton had said. He was going back to where it started—the message and the music... The new music had started in the courtyard of his hotel. She was sure of it, for it contained the same notes as the fountain there.

Sir Phillip's face turned white. "But where Gifford is often to be found."

"Gifford?" Maddie asked.

Lady Hadden spoke up. "Gifford hasn't the brains for a conspiracy."

Sir Phillip shrugged. "This is not the first time my notes have been disarranged, and Gifford always has the opportunity for that."

"The meeting must be in the courtyard at Prad's Hotel. We had tea there a week ago. I am sure that's what Leighton meant," Maddie said.

The clock chimed the half hour. Sir Phillip threw open a desk drawer.

"Very well. Go to bed. Do not concern yourself."

"But you are loading a pistol. How am I not to concern myself?"

Sir Phillip shook his head and left.

"Come, my dear, this is something neither one of us should be involved in."

Maddie let Lady Haddon lead her to her room numbly, while desperately trying to think how to get word to Leighton. It was half past eleven, and he might even now be sitting in that courtyard awaiting his death. And she might have just sent one of the conspirators there looking for him with a pistol. But if Sir Phillip was in on it, he would already know where the meeting was, wouldn't he? Perhaps not.

As soon as she was alone, she dug through her closet for her old dark cloak and threw it about her shoulders, then put out the lamp and slipped down the back stairs. Her escape from the garden was not so easy, for the gate still creaked, but she managed it and began to run. She lost herself among the last of the guests straggling away from the party.

She forced herself to be calm as she strode toward the hotel. Her sister's house was on the way. Perhaps Leighton's father was there. He could do something to stop this madness if she confronted him about his crime. She knocked loudly, wondering if she would be heeded at this time of night. To her surprise the door popped open.

"Maddie?"

Maddie rushed through the door before she realized it had been opened for her by her mother. She was still panting from running down the hill and blurted out, "Where is Lord Longbridge?" She was glad that she was in such a hurry, for it did not allow time for any awkwardness between them.

"I came home with Patience. He followed Leighton."

Maddie looked from her mother to her sister.

"You…you look frightened," Patience said.

"It's Leighton. I'm pretty sure he has gone off by himself to try to catch the spy."

"Spy?" her mother asked. "Oh, that. It is nothing."

"Nothing? Leighton got a note. I think it was meant for his father, setting up a meeting."

"That must be why William followed him, but there can be no danger. He means to—"

"No danger? But I thought Lord Longbridge was the spy."

"What? Are you mad?" her mother asked. "He is here to put an end to the plot."

"If that is true, Leighton might be safe. If not, he may be in the gravest danger."

"Do you really think it can be dangerous?" Her mother went to a trunk standing in the hall and brought out a case.

"There is no time to explain. I must find him."

"Wait." Her mother grabbed her arm. The contact was warm and poignant with memory. Maddie remembered the last time she had touched her mother. She'd found her crying in the garden and she would not say why.

"Please let me help," Rachel now said. Then she set about loading the gun, a thing Maddie had never seen her mother do before.

"It was that code he sent Leighton, the one in the music. Leighton got the same sort of message tonight. That's why I thought it was from Lord Longbridge."

"Did you decipher it?"

"No, he wouldn't give it to me. But I'm sure they are to meet in the courtyard at the hotel."

"Is there no one else we can confide in?" Patience asked. "Dr. Murray, perhaps?"

"I have already told far too many people. Lieutenant Reid knows but not the precise location. Leighton feels we can trust him. Sir Phillip is on his way, but I am not sure he is innocent, though he acts as though he is." She felt herself on the point of tears.

"Come, we do know *we* are to be trusted. We can take care of this ourselves."

"You are so different from before," Maddie said.

"That's what six years of love can do for a woman. All I needed was to know you do not hate me."

Maddie felt herself sway. Then she was in her mother's arms, and their embrace rivaled the one Leighton had bestowed on his father.

"I am so sorry I doubted you," she said.

"I should have taken you with me."

"No, Leighton needed me."

A brief knock at the door preceded Dierdra's desperate entrance. "What has happened? Why did you leave at night? Are you eloping? And where has Father gone with a pistol? Is he going to shoot Leighton?"

"We're not sure," Maddie said. "But how did you get here? You must go home."

"I can't go alone."

"Well, come with us, then." Rachel threw a cloak about her and caused Dierdra to blanch when she flourished her own pistol.

"But stay behind us," Maddie warned.

"I'm coming too," Patience said.

Dierdra was perfectly happy to bring up the rear of the expedition, though she continued to badger Patience with questions.

****

Leighton entered the dark courtyard and sat at one of the more obscure tables, not his favorite one near the fountain. Anyone who came in from the outside would have to use the gate at the bottom of the stone steps, and he would hear it creak. He questioned the wisdom of meeting in such a public place, but certainly no one inside the hotel could see him where he sat.

How odd. He felt perfectly at home here even though he could see only the splashing fountain by the moonlight. He was so proud of Maddie he could burst, not just her performance but her courage in accepting her mother in her new life when it went against everything she had been taught. He had a feeling that, no matter the challenge, Maddie would always be there for him.

There was no sound but the splashing of the water. Or was that the scrape of a shoe on stone? He stared into the dark corners of the courtyard, but he would have heard anyone enter from the hotel and certainly from the lower gate that let out onto the alley. Unless they were already here.

"Don't move," a voice grated as a knife point dug through the fabric of his coat to prick him near the spine. He would hear about that hole from Tibbs, if he survived.

"Mrs. Scrope-Nevins. You're a bit old to be waiting about in a garden in the middle of the night."

"Are you the Stone from America?"

"My name is Leighton Stone and, to be sure, I do have American connections."

"That is what I wanted to hear. And do they have an

238

interest in inconveniencing the present government?"

"They might. What did you have in mind?"

"Putting things right in France again. I have the ships in train. I need money, a small enough amount, and a promise from your government not to interfere."

"It is always easy not to interfere."

"You dance with me, boy. You have not said one thing to convince me—"

"Hold. You are both under arrest. And to think I avowed your innocence not an hour ago, Longbridge."

"Reid?" Leighton said gladly.

"You have said enough to make you gallows bait," Reid vowed as he came toward them with a pistol leveled.

Since Reid had not shot him on sight, the pistol did not worry him so much, but Leighton was still sitting rigidly, wondering at what moment Mrs. Scrope-Nevins might plunge the knife into his back or decide to cut his throat.

As Reid got close enough to check Leighton's pockets, he thought belatedly about the incriminating note.

The knife delivered a nick to Leighton, but Reid was the one in trouble, for in a lightning move the old woman had buried the short blade in the lieutenant's arm. He staggered backward without discharging the pistol, trying to reach the blade with his other hand, and fell into the pond, sloshing water over the flagstones.

Leighton leaped around the table. "What have you done?"

"Come, we must get away from here," the old lady said. "It's not safe."

That was an understatement. "No, he is drowning."

Reid was still underwater and thrashing. Leighton had no confidence he would not pass out and drown himself in no more than two feet of water.

He hauled Reid up onto the edge and helped him toward a chair, the knife still protruding from his biceps.

"What do you plan to do with him?" Scrope-Nevins asked.

Leighton was glad he realized she had picked up the pistol before he answered her. "Nothing for the moment, but he might be useful later."

"Let me dispatch him now."

"When I have been to such pains to save him?" Leighton turned his back on her, then whipped around and grabbed the pistol, wrenching it upward from her grasp and pulling her off her feet in the process. He caught the old woman in his other arm and coiled it around her, taking a multitude of kicks in his shins and hearing some colorful profanity, mostly in French.

Dr. Murray came hurrying out of the hotel with his bag and made Reid lie back. "I was watching from your window," he said as he used his handkerchief to stop the bleeding. "Need any help, Leighton?"

"Only for Reid, but she is stronger than I thought. She had better stop biting me, or I'll have no compunction about whacking her over the head with this thing."

"You can prove nothing," she growled. "I gave nothing in writing. It will be my word against—"

"Yes, I know, a music master's."

"And a surgeon in the employ of the army," Murray added.

"Reid, you are supposed to say something reassuring," Leighton rasped out as the old woman struggled in his arms.

Reid gasped as the knife was extracted. "You had me convinced you were making a deal with her."

"I was leading her on to get her to reveal her contact," Leighton growled. "You might have waited."

"Very well. It will be her word against one of Wellington's staff."

"See. Ow." Leighton finally put the pistol on the table and pinned both the woman's wrists behind her. Murray left Reid to hold his own compress while he came to bind her hands with linen strips.

"Thank you," Leighton said. "How is Reid?"

"It missed the artery, though it nicked a vein. He'll live. Another scar for your collection, Reid."

"Happy day. I need a brandy. This is my first experience of nearly being killed by an octogenarian."

"I demand to see a magistrate," Mrs. Scrope-Nevins said.

"You are awfully eager to get out of this courtyard," Murray said. "I wonder who else is coming."

"Gag her," Reid said. "We don't want her giving us away if there is anyone else involved. Sorry, Stone. I leapt to conclusions."

"There are more than two parties, I figure," Leighton said as he crammed his handkerchief into the old woman's mouth and tied it in place with a strip of linen. He dragged her behind a shrub and dropped her there. "She's the contact with the ships, unless I miss my guess, to carry Napoleon and his men away from Elba. So *the money* is still missing, as is the information on the location of the fleet."

"Why would she need that?" Murray asked as he bundled the used linen away and helped Reid to a concealed chair.

"To avoid the British navy, one must know where it will be and where it will not be."

"So are we waiting for two others?" Reid asked, his breath hissing through his teeth as the doctor deposited him on a chair.

"Yes, I fear so." Leighton was beginning to wonder what he was going to do if one of them was his father.

The gate creaked. The man who walked into the moonlit courtyard did not seem at all perturbed by the quantity of water splashed on the flagstones nor by the darker splashes of blood.

"Fath— Uncle!"

"Leighton? What are you doing here? I think that message was meant for me."

"Not minding my own business. What are you doing here?"

"I came to meet a British spy. I believe you have her there under restraint. But who spilled whose blood?"

"She stabbed Reid," Leighton said as his father came over to have a look, completely ignoring the pistol Murray was pointing at him.

"Yes, yes, I know," Leighton said. "It looks bad, three grown men not able to manage one old woman, but she did take us by surprise."

"I am the American connection, the American Stone, if you will." He got out his cigar case but hesitated. "If we are still waiting for someone, I don't suppose I will have time to smoke."

"No," Leighton said in a strangled voice.

Reid was still panting and holding the cloth to his arm. "In the name of the King, I arrest—"

"You are in no position to arrest anyone," William

Stone said as he pointed the unlit cigar at Reid. "Hear me out. I have been asked by my government—that is, the American government—to ferret out this conspiracy and squelch it. This woman with her conniving is a danger to the peace process. Above all, we want no scandal and no hint that America was involved in this nonsense in any way."

"Brave words," Dr. Murray said, "which you might have composed once you saw we had her captured."

"My orders," William said, producing a packet from his inside coat pocket.

The paper crinkled in Murray's hands as he tried to read by moonlight. "I shall have to take you at your word until later. So America will have no part in this, but that does not solve it. If Leighton guesses aright, someone is still selling England out."

"And it could be Sir Phillip Haddon," Reid said.

Another shriek of the gate hinges sent them all scrambling for hiding places. Leighton's father sheltered behind the same bush with Leighton and gave a low laugh at the trussed Mrs. Scrope-Nevins. "This is almost as good as a play," he whispered. At the last moment he flitted like a shadow to a column in the colonnade near the top of the steps.

But it was not Haddon. Leighton saw Haddon's cousin and heir, Gifford, come nervously into the moonlight with his hand in his pocket. He advanced past them and was peering into the far corner when Mrs. Scrope-Nevins ground Leighton's hand under her heel, causing him to grunt in pain.

Gifford turned to flee, but Lord Longbridge blocked his way and faced a pistol aimed at his head.

"Out of my way, or I will use this," Gifford warned.

"That little thing? You should buy your pistols from America."

Leighton could see now that his father had a much larger weapon leveled at Gifford's stomach. Where had he secreted such a pistol?

"Well, that is the Navy connection," Reid said. "Have we got everyone now?"

Leighton abandoned the bound woman to advance across the courtyard toward Gifford. He should be able to draw the man's fire away from his father.

The gate did not creak, but there were stealthy steps coming up the stairs. Haddon must have left it open. Leighton and his father glanced at each other. Surely no one else could be involved.

"Be silent or I will fire. I will kill at least one of you." Gifford backed toward the stairs, his eyes fixed on Leighton's father as he positioned himself by the gatepost.

The soft patter of female steps gave Leighton an uneasy feeling. Sure enough, Maddie in her old cloak appeared in the archway, with Patience and Rachel behind her. And if he was not mistaken, that was Dierdra looking over their shoulders.

"Rachel, go back," his father shouted, but Gifford grabbed Maddie about the waist and held the gun to her head before Leighton could react.

Then he froze. Resourceful as he considered himself, he did not know what to do. "Gifford, you can accomplish nothing by holding Maddie."

"I can make my escape."

"Where would you go?"

"France. There is at least one ship in Bristol ready to sail to the continent."

"And I carry enough money on me to provision it," Leighton said.

"What?" chorused several voices.

"But only if you let Maddie go. Take me instead."

"I don't need to let her go to make you do what I want."

"I'd be less trouble to you than Maddie."

"Less trouble?" Maddie protested. She slumped as though in a dead faint and elbowed Gifford in the groin, giving Rachel the opening to wound him in the shoulder with her pistol.

Leighton leaped toward Gifford, grabbed the pistol from his hand, and lifted Maddie to her feet. "See, I told you I'd be less trouble."

"Oh, is that what you meant?" Maddie laughed.

"Yes, my dear, you would never make a manageable hostage."

"I think I'm out of bandages," Dr. Murray said. He coughed at the powder smoke hanging in the air.

Gifford was moaning theatrically, making not the slightest impression on Leighton's father.

"Good shooting, Rachel," he said as she went to hug him.

"Maddie, are you all right?" Leighton hugged her tighter.

In the relative calm, Mrs. Scrope-Nevins had regained her feet and scuttled toward the door into the hotel, but Reid picked up his pistol and stopped her. "I'll have no scruples to shoot you down, old woman. You would have sold me and my fellows into war again."

She stopped just as a brace of footmen emerged from the hotel with Sir Phillip. Reid directed them to hold her.

"Dierdra, what are you doing here?" Leighton asked.

"I followed Maddie. I thought you were eloping."

"Not a bad idea, but not tonight, I think. I'm afraid poor Reid has been wounded."

"Wounded?" Dierdra rushed to him and knelt to add her insignificant handkerchief to the padding on his arm.

Reid smiled at her. "You are an amazing girl."

"Imagine that," Leighton's father said. "You girls coming to our rescue."

"Dierdra," her father said, "how did you get involved in this?"

"Never mind that now. Did you hear, Father? Gifford is a traitor. I don't still have to marry him, do I?"

"Certainly not."

"And Lieutenant Reid is a hero."

Sir Haddon nodded. "So I noticed."

"Maddie, how did you all get here?" Leighton demanded.

"We were in such a hurry we had to bring her with us. Why didn't you tell me?"

"I didn't want you in danger."

"Don't ever keep something like this from me again."

"I should hope not. If I ever get another coded message, I'll burn it."

Chapter Twenty-Two

"So how did you get involved in the plot to free Napoleon?" Leighton asked as Maddie, his father, Rachel, and Patience were enjoying tea in Patience's drawing room.

His father set down his cup as though it was going to be a long story. "Mrs. Scrope-Nevins petitioned a whole list of landowners for contributions, at least that is what I heard. She knew many Americans had French sympathies, but most of them would not get involved. I went to the government to see if they knew what she was doing and if they wanted to prevent her."

Rachel looked at her husband proudly. "They asked him to investigate the plot and scotch it if he could. They already were trying to make peace, and any American involvement, even privately, in such a scheme could have ruined that."

Maddie smiled at her. "Also, it jumped with your own inclination to come to Bath."

"Yes, I had to talk to Patience to see if we could rescue you somehow. I had no idea Leighton was already working on it."

"And making slow progress," he confessed. "If I had not always been blurting my suspicions out to Maddie, we might have run off and been married by now."

Patience cast him a frown. "But then the plot might have succeeded."

"Possibly," Lord Longbridge said. "I went to Bristol to check on those ships Mrs. Scrope-Nevins mentioned. Indeed, she had engaged three ships, but they were waiting for money so they could be provisioned." He took up his replenished cup and drank, as the others speculated on possible outcomes.

"Why couldn't Gifford have supplied the money?" Maddie asked. "He seemed to have plenty. And if it comes to that, why would he sell out his country? He is a coward and stupid, but why run the risk?"

"Reid answered that for me," Leighton supplied. "He checked in London and Gifford is heavily in debt. He has a penchant for gambling but no skill. He was hoping Mrs. Scrope-Nevins would pay him for information."

"Well, that explains most of it, except why you sent the code on to Leighton." Maddie wanted to hear Lord Longbridge's side of it.

"If I'd had any idea that Mrs. Scrope-Nevins could be dangerous or that she had an accomplice, I never would have involved Leighton. But I couldn't resist the chance to see if he could still solve the sort of puzzles he enjoyed as a boy. I'd no idea he'd been doing that sort of work these last few years."

"Or that Maddie would be the one to solve it." Leighton put his arm around her. "What finally linked the code to you in my mind was the scent of your tobacco."

"Ah, I had not even thought of that."

"Leighton guessed it was a substitution but tried the wrong way to get the variations. I simply turned it on its head. But Mrs. Scrope-Nevins never worked out that code. You did."

"Yes, when I was asked to expose her, I sent her the code, not such a difficult one when you have the key. She loved the intrigue of it. When I sent word of my plans to come to Bath, she thought she had snared me."

"I would never have pursued the decoding if my rooms had not been searched," Leighton said. "Reid admitted to that."

Maddie nodded. "And it must have been he who disarranged your room at Marsden House."

"He apologized. He and Dr. Murray have been investigating this plot for months, based on gossip coming out of Bath. They were getting frantic to expose the culprit. Now that I think of it, we were lucky not to get shot for our pains."

Rachel reached for her daughter's hand. "We were torn about whether to tell you or not. When Patience said Leighton was courting you, we thought perhaps there was no need, but I so wanted to see you again, to hope that you would forgive me if you knew."

"I'm glad now Leighton exposed you. It was a shock, to be sure, but he is right. You had no choice but to go to America. After so much sorrow, I am glad you are happy now."

"I had you girls to comfort me. That was worth everything. And you are going to come for a visit."

"Yes," Leighton agreed. "As soon as British ships can legally run to America."

"And that's why you farmed me out to the Haddons," Maddie said to Patience. "I was so angry with you I could have spit."

"If they wanted to keep themselves secret, I thought it best they stay here."

"As soon as Maddie went to Haddon House, we

removed here from the hotel," said Rachel.

"I thought it would be safer," Patience put in. "There would be less chance you would bump into them. I didn't count on Leighton invading the second drawing room."

Leighton chuckled. "Odd we chose the same hotel."

"Not odd. It has a stable where one can rent a horse."

"Ah."

Patience's butler opened the double doors into the drawing room. "Lady Longbridge and Mr. Westlake."

Leighton saw his mother come in with her nose in the air and two bright spots of color on her cheeks. She was carrying a ridiculous parasol and took a seat without being invited as Patience looked nervously from her to her father.

Westlake's gaze raked Rachel, and Leighton could see her wilting like a flower even though his father pressed her hand tighter.

Maddie stood up between her mother and father in a shielding way. "I think you should sit down…sir. This may take some time." She took his sleeve and conducted him to a chair by Leighton's mother. The man looked shocked. They all looked shocked.

"Constance Madeline. You condone this…sin?"

Maddie turned to him. "Since I have the experience of keeping house for you and know how unappreciative, overbearing, and downright nasty you can be—and you a man of the clergy—yes, I condone her behavior since you discarded her—threw her out of the house, in fact."

"So you know," Leighton's mother said.

His father chuckled. "Yes, your lay has been rumbled."

"It would have been better if you had not returned," Lady Longbridge said.

"We would not have," Rachel said, "if Horace had kept his word. She turned to her husband, drawing strength from Maddie's defense of her. "He promised to let Maddie go to live with Patience. He lied about that."

Leighton's father nodded. "We would have come back sooner if the war had not prevented it."

"I wanted to make sure at least one of my daughters was raised correctly."

"Oh, really?" Patience asked. "I am sorry now I let you bully me into covering your lie."

"Lie? In my heart I felt my wife was dead. The blame rests on these two sinners."

Leighton's father chuckled again. "You may not have killed your wife, Westlake, but you certainly killed your marriage and her love for you. You have no idea what it's like to have someone gnaw away at every good intention, every noble thought till there is nothing left but a desperate hunger for escape."

"And I suppose you do," Leighton's mother challenged.

"Yes, I do know what that is like." His look at her was not one of hatred but of sadness.

"I did not drive you away."

"You underrate yourself, my dear. You most certainly did."

"I did not think you would go. I told you we could make some arrangement. You could have had your mistress on the side. You could have taken her away and kept her on your estate in America, as you have done."

This produced a shocked gasp from everyone, including Maddie's father. Westlake stared at Lady Longbridge as though he did not know her.

"However, I now see the wisdom of divorce. We

should proceed with it."

"What?" Leighton stood up. "What has changed since you went to London? You've had an offer, haven't you? And for you to marry would be bigamy. Yet you can't give that as a reason. You've been trapped by your own ingenuity, Mother. This must be a pretty big fish, for you to give up being Lady Longbridge."

"Never mind who he is. I want a divorce."

"And I should like to oblige, but the situation is out of our hands." Leighton's father slowly lit one of his cigars, and Leighton remembered how much his mother hated them.

"What do you mean?"

"After I received your letter informing me that I was dead, I drafted a codicil to my own will, leaving my American holdings to William Stone, my illegitimate half-brother. It was properly witnessed and dated before my death. I cannot come back and neither can Rachel. You saw to that."

His mother turned to Leighton. "You knew about this?"

"Yes, but I had no time or inclination to look into the bequest. I'd just lost my father. What did I care for land in America? Besides, divorce is only by a Bill of Parliament, and for that the husband has to be alive and the other man convicted."

"This isn't fair."

Leighton sighed. "As I see it, you have trapped yourselves."

"But they are happy, as though they were married," his mother protested.

"I'm pretty sure they are married in the only way that matters. And they are far happier than when they were legally married. But the two of you have condemned yourselves to lives of solitude."

"I suppose you will give the living to someone else," Westlake said, looking much older than he had when he entered the room.

"Certainly not. I wish to see you live out your punishment."

"How dare you preach to me?"

"How dare you preach anything but forgiveness?" Leighton asked. "You provoked the situation. I can only hope time will teach you the lessons your family could not when you had the keeping of them."

"What am I supposed to do now?" Lady Longbridge wailed. "I am neither married nor a widow."

"Maddie and I are getting married. We invite you to stay for the wedding. Beyond that, your situation has not changed, except that you may have your own house in London. Much good may it do you."

"Stay for the wedding?" his mother asked. "To the daughter of that woman?"

"Maddie is my daughter too," Westlake said.

"You—you side with them?"

"When you proposed the scheme to me, I knew it was wrong. I knew I would be punished for it. But I saw no other way. Call Rachel dead? Yes, I was doing that already. But you left yourself a way out that I did not see. You could always have your husband come back from the dead if you needed him. Even if you only needed to sue for separation. But that escape has been taken away. So you are punished as well."

"Are you telling me you condone this misalliance?"

"Which misalliance?" Maddie asked. "Mother and William, or Leighton and me?"

"You and Leighton, you scheming girl."

Westlake stood. "I…am staying for the wedding."

"Very well, you can go to the devil for all I care. Get back to Longbridge on your own." Lady Longbridge rose and stalked from the room.

Westlake stood up as well, and Patience conducted him out. Leighton wondered if she would recommend Prad's Hotel.

"Well, you got your way," Maddie said. "Permission to marry me."

Leighton chuckled. "I hope I don't do anything else to upset you before we get that license."

"I might take Dierdra's advice and lock you up until then."

His father rose and pulled Rachel to her feet. "I can tell this will soon get maudlin, and I wouldn't want to hamper romance, so we are off to the Pump Room. Try to stay out of any more conspiracies, both of you."

"What?" Leighton asked. "I wasn't the one—"

"Let them go," Maddie said.

"But he is the one who dragged us into the spy plot to begin with."

She stopped his complaint with a kiss, then rested her head on his chest.

"Your father was funning, wasn't he, about the codicil?" she asked.

"No, but he could resurrect himself and still keep the American lands."

"So he *could* divorce her now, but he won't. Why?"

"No, he could not, because that would require another man to blame. He could let her separate from him by claiming mistreatment at his hands, but then everything would have to come out, though I doubt it's the scandal that concerns him. Probably he just wants to save some other poor fellow from what he endured. Do you mind so much if she lives in the North Wing?"

"No, of course not. I almost feel sorry for her."

"At least it looks as if we may make peace with your father. That is far more important," Leighton observed.

"What a lot of plots and coils we have faced."

"And I have neglected you terribly these last few days."

"I was just thinking, Leighton. If it would take only half a dozen ships to rescue Napoleon and restore him to France, shouldn't the government be warned it's a possibility?"

"I am quite sure Reid covered it in his report."

"If Dierdra has let him write it. She is supervising his care at Marsden House."

"Don't worry. It would never have worked anyway. A thousand men cannot retake a country."

"If you say so. But you have been wrong before," Maddie reminded him.

"That is why I need you so much." He tightened his hug. "We solve problems best when we work together."

"Promise me it will always be so, no matter what we face."

"That you will always be at my side is my one wish, whether we are sailing to visit family in America, or riding the fields at Longbridge, or even burying a dead cat. I always want you by me."

She raised her face. He dipped his head and touched his lips to hers as though they were sacred and he was only tasting because he didn't think he deserved them. When she deepened the kiss, need and giving washed back and forth between them like an exchange of some life-giving element.

As she held onto his strong frame, she felt for the first time as though she held the future and not the past. As though she held already their children and all the amazing hours they would have because she had forgiven him and not turned her back on happiness.

He laced his fingers with hers, and she looked at their joined hands. "Do you think it's true that the vows we make to each other in private are as binding as the public ones?"

"I think so, and I also think that love, true love, is more binding than any document. We are one, Maddie, as we were meant to be from the start."

"I have been wrong on occasion too. I am glad you did not give up but convinced me forgiveness is entwined with love." She raised her face for his kiss, leaving all doubts behind her.

Epilogue

In the spring of the next year, before Maddie and Leighton had been delivered of their first child, Napoleon did indeed escape Elba with a half dozen ships and a thousand men. His old army turned its back on the Royalists and flocked to his banner, pitching Europe into a war that would end at the village of Waterloo in Belgium. Though Leighton followed events with the utmost interest, he realized the new conflict had nothing to do with codes and did not feel tempted to offer his services again.

A word about the author...

Barbara Jean Miller has mentored in the Writing Popular Fiction Masters Program at Seton Hill University since its inception in 1999. She writes in several genres but her favorite is historical romantic suspense. She calls them action/adventure romances with the heroine sharing in the struggles and rescue in equal part with the hero. These struggles often involve mysteries and horses.

Barb lives with her husband and pets on an ancient farm in Western Pennsylvania which contributes authentic settings to her novels.

https://barbarajeanmiller.substack.com